I0734279

綺麗な妖怪

KIREINA YŌKAI

Z.R. Billings

Title page artwork by Marlee Suddarth
Artwork by Renni Yu
Typography by Jportrait
Edited by Michael Blundell

Second Edition: February 2026

ISBN: 978-1-7373471-9-4

Printed in the United States of America

Arial Typeface used in *Kireina Yōkai.*

*For Brandon and Matthew, thank you for allowing me to be
a part of your story for all these years.*

And for the first time, I felt like he actually saw me….

STAGE 1:
DENIAL

"Hey, Takahashi," Minori warily greeted as his eyes met with Daichi Takahashi's. Daichi jumped as he looked up from the ground and Minori came into view.

"Saito?" Daichi slowly asked, wide-eyed in disbelief. He quickly glanced around him as other students passed by, paying them no mind.

"Pretty weird, huh?" Minori asked, looking at the other students exiting the school.

"This–This can't be real," Daichi replied, rubbing his eyes with the palms of his hands.

"Yeah, that's what I've been telling myself, too," Minori sighed. "But the more time that passes, the more I believe it," he added as he looked around at the passersby.

Daichi's eyes readjusted, and sure enough, Minori still remained before him, enveloped in a ghastly blue, like he had been drained of all color that wasn't a shade of azure.

"H-How is this possible?" Daichi stammered, gripping the strap of his book bag.

"I've been wondering the same thing," Minori answered, studying the back of his hand as he held it up to the sky. "I just woke up and this was me."

Daichi took notice of some of his fellow classmates giving him looks. He politely smiled and gave a gentle wave before walking away; this probably wasn't the best place to commune with the presumed dead.

"I take it no one else has been able to see you yet," Daichi commented as he made his way home with Minori floating beside him.

"Not yet," Minori replied. "Believe me, you're the last person I expected to be able to."

"Had your plan been to just wander around school till someone took notice?" Daichi asked.

"That was the plan," Minori lamented with a sigh.

"I see. Did you already check with your family?" Daichi asked.

"Yeah, they were the first people I tried," Minori frowned.

"How long have you been like this?" Daichi inquired.

"A month?" Minori replied with a question of his own as he looked up at the sky. "Thing is, when you're dead, time just seems to blend together. When was my funeral?"

"I'm not sure," Daichi admitted. "A month ago?"

"So then, about a month, I guess," Minori presumed with his hand to his chin. "Sorry to put this all on you, Takahashi, but I could really use your help," he sheepishly smiled.

"That's alright," Daichi replied. "But I'm not sure how much help I'm going to really be. I don't know much about ghosts or spirits."

"Then that makes two of us," Minori chuckled.

"I'm really sorry, Saito," Daichi frowned, facing forward.

"Death is just another path we all must take," Minori breathed, looking to the horizon.

"You're taking this rather well," Daichi replied. "If I were you, I would totally be freaking out."

"You think?" Minori laughed, looking over to the young man beside him.

"No doubt," Takashi smiled. *You're amazing, Minori,* he quietly thought to himself.

"Well, I did have about a month to come to terms with it," Minori explained.

"Shouldn't you have moved on, then?" Daichi asked, a little skeptical.

"Yeah, I suppose you're probably right, huh?" Minori smiled, appearing a little embarrassed.

13

"So something has to be keeping you here," Daichi concluded, thinking it over in his head.

"Well, there was a bunch of stuff I had wanted to do before I died," Minori admitted as he studied the ground, passing through a bike rack as he floated along. "Well, then, the solution is simple..." Daichi replied, coming to a stop.

"Hmm?" Minori asked, his head snapping to the brown-haired youth.

"We just need to do those things!" Daichi grinned, sliding his hands into his pockets.

"You think?" Minori questioned, not convinced. "Don't most people die with regrets?"

"I suppose," Daichi softly agreed, looking away, towards the sky. The two of them stood in silence for a moment. "But I want to help you, Saito, and this seems like the best shot I have at doing so. I've spent my life avoiding people for the most part. I've always just been more comfortable on my own, with my nose in a book or my eyes on some sort of screen, you know? I just never felt like I fit in with anyone at school, let alone my class; you and I don't really know each other all that well, but you always went out of your way to be nice to me, so if I can help you with this, then I owe it to you to do so."

"Takahashi...you don't owe me anything," Minori quietly replied.

"Truth is, Saito, I honestly regretted not going out of my way to get to know you better," Daichi smiled, ignoring Minori's comment. "So, as your friend, I'm going to make sure you get to the other side."

"Thanks, Takahashi," Minori smiled.

So we made a list…

One thing became two.

Four became six.

And before we knew it.....

15

STAGE 2:

Bargaining

"Is that everything?" Daichi asked, looking at the collection of words on the notebook in front of him.

Minori thought it over, placing his hand to his chin as he stared up at the ceiling. "Nothing else comes to mind."

"Alright then," Daichi nodded, inspecting the list of things to do, "that leaves the final count at nine. Kind of small, if you ask me. Are you sure there's nothing else you wanted to do before you died?"

Minori laughed, "What can I say, I'm a simple man."

Daichi reviewed the list of things in front of him. None of it was anything special; they were all rather mundane, actually–things your average teenager has likely done. Nothing on it seemed like anything Minori hadn't already done before, with a few exceptions.

"Alright," Daichi breathed. "So number one, we have 'go to a hot spring.' You've never done that before?"

"No," Minori laughed. "No, music has kept me pretty busy. I never had the time."

"Huh, I knew you were in a band, but I guess I never realized it was that serious," Daichi admitted.

"Yeah, we were actually starting to really get a buzz going. Talk about ironic, huh?" Minori chuckled.

"You sure you don't have any regrets there?" Daichi asked.

"Regrets?" Minori asked, appearing a little puzzled. "No, I gave it my all. My only regrets are on that page in front of you."

"There's nothing else you wanted to have done with it?" Daichi asked, not convinced.

"Well, sure, in theory, but it's hard to miss something you never had," Minori replied. "What I mean is, I have no idea how the band would have turned out with me in it. Sure, it *could* have been something incredible–sold-out arenas, meet-and-greets–but it could have easily been something that didn't go anywhere, and I could have dropped it when I went to university. The things on that list are all things I had hoped to do—more or less planned to do—when the time felt right."

"I guess that's fair," Daichi softly replied, picking up his notebook from the floor and giving the list another look. "You want to go to a festival? Our school has had more than one of those. You're telling me you never attended a single one?"

"I mean a real festival, not one put on by a bunch of high schoolers," Minori warmly laughed.

"You've never attended a festival?" Daichi asked, looking up from the floor at Minori.

"Sure, I have. I just would have liked to have gone to one more," he explained.

"Alright, that's simple enough. Gion Matsuri will be coming up soon here, so we can go to that," Daichi said as he thought it over in his head. *Okay, that's two more or less down. Shouldn't be hard to find a hot spring we can go to, and the festival is just around the corner. Easy. It'll be a long trip, but if it makes Saito happy, then it's worth it,* Daichi quietly pondered to himself as he considered the logistics. *Besides, I've never been to Kyoto before. Would be cool to finally get to see it.*

"You okay, Takahashi?" Minori asked, breaking Daichi's trance.

"Oh, sorry, I was just thinking," Daichi smiled as he ruffled the hair on the back of his head. "Okay, so number three," he returned his gaze to the notebook in his hand, "you want to visit the Fushimi Inari Shrine. That's simple enough."

"I thought it would be cool," Minori smiled.

"That's in Kyoto, right?" Daichi inquired, looking up from the list for clarification. "Yeah, which is why I haven't gotten to see it yet," Minori replied. *That makes another trip to Kyoto,* Daichi quietly assessed, his eyes fixed on the page where it read 'visit Fushimi Inari Shrine.' "Alright, number...four, you want to go to an aquarium; any one in particular?" he asked, looking back up at Minori.

Minori thought for a moment, placing his hand to his chin. "I hadn't put much thought into it. There was one in Shinagawa that my friend Kurashita told me about."

"Alright, that works!" Daichi chimed. "Do you happen to remember the name?"

Minori frowned, appearing to be doing his best to remember. "Ah, no, I can't seem to recall."

"That's alright. Shinagawa narrows it down. Maybe I can find them at school and ask them," Daichi smiled before writing 'Shinagawa' at the end of number four. *Onto number five,* he silently proclaimed, his eyes moving down the list. "Number five, marathon every Studio Ghibli film."

"Always meant to watch them. I figured a marathon would be a good way to get caught up," Minori sheepishly laughed, avoiding eye contact with Daichi.

"Alright, that's easy enough," Daichi nodded, taking out his cell phone from his front pocket; he clicked an indented button on its side, illuminating its screen and bringing it to life. Seeing this, he quickly slid his thumb up against it, unlocking it. "Let's see here," he mumbled as he searched how many Studio Ghibli films there were. "Looks like...nineteen."

"Nineteen?" Minori exclaimed, completely flabbergasted.

"Yup, nineteen. Going to be a full day of cinema," Daichi replied, looking over all the different films. "Should be fun, though," he smiled up at Minori. "I haven't seen them all, and most of the ones I have seen, I saw when I was little, so it'll be nice to finally rewatch them." Daichi turned off his phone and set it on the floor, his eyes returning to his notebook. "Okay, so number six, see an orchestra perform. Any group in particular?" Daichi inquired once again, looking to Minori for clarification.

Minori shook his head, "So long as they can do the pieces they're playing justice, I don't much care who it is."

Spoken like a true musician, Daichi quietly admired as he nodded his head, his eyes returning back to his lap.

"That one might take some work, but I'm sure we can find at least one group performing. Number seven, you said ride a ferris wheel...seems kind of odd," Daichi laughed, "but we can do that. Number eight, easy enough, watch the sunset on a beach. And last one, number nine, take a cross-country trip."

The two sat quietly for a moment, Daichi pondering the logistics of the bucket list.

"What do you think?" Minori asked, lying down on Daichi's small, twin-sized, bed.

"It seems pretty doable," Daichi replied. "The cross-country trip is going to be difficult, but I think if that's the hardest thing we have to worry about, we'll be okay."

"You don't think it's too much?" Minori asked, sitting up and turning to face Daichi. "It's your bucket list," Daichi shrugged. "I think by most people's standards, you're actually aiming really low."

"You think so?" Minori asked, thinking it over.

"Just leave it to me! I got this, Saito!" Daichi exclaimed, pointing to himself with his thumb.

"My life is in your capable hands," Minori fondly smiled.

"I won't let you down," Daichi beamed as he leaned back on his hands.

"I'm sure you won't," Minori nodded.

Over the next two months, we got to know each other pretty well, and knocked a couple things off my bucket list while we were at it.

We watched ALL nineteen Studio Ghibli films.

We ended up having to do it over the course of an entire weekend, but we managed to do it. Turns out Daichi is a bit of a movie snob. Maybe that's the real reason he hadn't seen most of them...

We rode a ferris wheel together. His friends looked at him like he was crazy when he said he wanted to ride alone, ha, ha, ha. But it made me happy that it was just the two of us.

It was nice seeing him with others. At school, he always looked so alone. It's good to know he has people to hang out with.

He took me to see a proper orchestra play. He even went so far as to buy two tickets so the seat beside him was open. I think it may very well have been the best night of my...well, 'life.'

What else.......

Oh! We got to visit a hot spring! In hindsight, I suppose it was a bit of a silly request, seeing as I couldn't quite enjoy the best part, but the company made it worth it.

We did end up visiting the aquarium in Shinagawa. It was called Aqua Park, in case you were wondering. Kurashita looked so confused when Daichi marched up to her asking the name of the place, ha, ha, ha. It was actually kind of adorable...She actually offered to go with him. Can you believe it? Ha, ha, ha. Thankfully for yours truly, he politely declined, like a true gentleman. It was wonderful. For any fellow ghosts out there looking for a date—I mean, things to do with your mortal friends, aquariums are great. You can see the water shows without fear of getting wet, and since everything is behind glass anyway, you experience it just as those who are living. Though I shall admit, I tried to walk through the glass a number of times to see if I could manage it. Plus, it was nice seeing Daichi laugh at my attempts. Perhaps that's the real reason I tried it at every exhibit we encountered.

That left only four more things…and a whole summer to do them.

STAGE 3:

DEPRESSION

Daichi and Minori sat beside one another on a peninsula of smooth rocks that stretched out from Ohara Beach into the sea. The sky wasn't yet ablaze with light, but it wouldn't be much longer now.

"Finally, summer vacation," Daichi smiled as he looked out at the horizon, his legs crossed in front of him and his arms resting upon his knees. "You know what that means?"

"No more homework?" Minori smiled.

"No," Daichi began with a laugh. "Summer festivals!"

"Oh, yeah, of course, I knew that," Minori replied, appearing to have been caught off guard.

"Yeah, sure, you did," Daichi teased.

"Hey, Takahashi?" Minori asked, changing the mood to something a little more somber with just the tone of his voice.

"What is it? Did I say something wrong?" Daichi asked, looking over at the corporeal boy beside him.

"I just wanted to thank you for everything you've done for me: the concert, taking me to a hot spring, riding the ferris wheel. I'm sure it's been difficult to help me and keep up with your studies," Minori explained.

"It's alright. It's been nice," Daichi smiled, softly chuckling. "Hanging out with you sure beats hanging out alone in my room playing video games."

"Wow, really?" Minori quietly asked.

"Positive," Daichi nodded, returning his eyes to the sea. "The past two months have been the best two months of my life, believe it or not. I can't remember the last time I had this much fun. Don't get me wrong, Hayashi and Matsuda are great and all, but hanging out with them isn't the same thing as when we hang out, ya know?"

"Absolutely," Minori warmly smiled.

"I only wish we could have all hung out together

sooner!" Daichi grinned, looking at Minori.

"Me too," Minori warily sighed.

Shit, maybe I shouldn't have said that. Stupid. Idiot, Daichi violently chastised himself. "But you know what they say, 'Better late than never,'" Daichi quietly added, looking away from Minori's face. He couldn't bear to see him appearing so sullen, even if it was justified.

"I guess that's true, huh?" Minori sighed, looking out at the horizon. "I only wish I hadn't been so late. I hope you can forgive me. I guess I had just always thought there'd be more time."

"I should be the one apologizing, Saito, not you!" Daichi quickly protested, his whole body moving in opposition.

"Hey, Takahashi...can you just call me Minori?" the pale spirit asked, not taking his eyes off the water.

"Okay, but only under one condition!" Daichi replied.

Dammit, am I going to cry right now? he silently asked himself as he began to feel his throat tighten. "What is it?" Minori asked, turning to look into Daichi's glistening, emerald eyes.

"You have to call me Daichi!" the meek, mousy-haired boy shouted back. Minori was clearly taken aback and for a moment sat silently before smiling.

"Okay, deal, Daichi," he quietly replied.

I wish we could have lived in that moment forever…

The sky was beautiful…

I'll cherish the memory, so long as I exist, even if it's not along the same plane as you…

The image is baked into my soul. Even now, I can recall the colors of the light, the shining of the sea, and the smell of the air…

And your astonishing emerald eyes.

I'll never forget them.
Ever.

I promise….

"Was it everything you had hoped for?" Daichi asked as he laid in his bed, looking up at his ceiling, the light of the moon gently caressing his room.

"And more," Minori happily smiled as he laid on a shikibuton Daichi had needlessly gotten into a habit of setting up for him every night. "I have never been to Isumi before."

"It was cool getting to see the Obama Hachiman Shrine, too, even if it was a bit of a walk," Daichi said, remembering how awesome the shrine looked tucked away in its home on high, overlooking the sea.

"Yeah, but because we did that, we also got to see Ohara Port," Minori replied.

"Yeah, I guess that's true," Daichi smiled. "I've never seen so many boats in one place before, not that I've seen a boat in person before anyway, heh, heh, heh."

"Me either," Minori chuckled. "I've been to the railway museum, though."

"Huh, how was it?" Daichi asked.

"It was okay. I went such a long time ago, though. I was just a kid," Minori replied.

"You want to go check it out together?" Daichi asked, rolling onto his side to peer down at his ghostly roommate.

"Huh?" Minori peeped. "Would you want to go to something like that?"

"Sure, why not?" Daichi chuckled. "It's here in Saitama anyway, right?"

"Well, sure, but it's not on the list," Minori softly replied, still appearing surprised.

"So? The list is more like a guideline than actual rule, right? Last I checked, there were no rules against adding on to it," Daichi argued.

"Well, if you don't mind…" Minori quietly replied.

33

"Then, that settles it! We'll definitely go check it out!" Daichi eagerly chimed, returning to lying on his back.

And like that, the list grew by one.

"Wow, Minori really sold this place short," Daichi beamed as he stood in what one could call the main observation hall of the railway museum—or in the museum's own words, the 'Rolling Stock Station,' an enormous space in building one that housed rail cars from throughout Japan's history.

"You sure have been talking about Saito a lot these past few months," Haru replied with his hands in his pockets. "I had no idea you two had been so close."

"Yeah, me neither," Matsu added.

"Oh, sorry, I guess he's just been on my mind a lot lately," Daichi explained, holding back his laughter as he looked at Minori standing with the two other boys.

"It's alright. I only meant had I known, I would have offered my condolences sooner," Haru elucidated.

"Yeah, man," Matsu frowned. "The way you've been talking about him…it must be hard for you, what happened and all, if that makes any sense."

"It's alright," Daichi replied, his face softening. "No one could have predicted the accident."

"Still," Matsu mumbled, rubbing the back of his neck as he avoided eye contact.

"You guys were his friends, too," Daichi politely rebutted.

"I don't think anyone wasn't," Haru half-heartedly smiled.

"Yeah," Matsu sighed. "He seemed to get along with everyone."

"He certainly did, huh?" Daichi asked, thinking it over.

"Being kind to everyone never cost me anything," Minori replied as he inspected one of the nearby train cars.

"You know, Minori told me something once," Daichi softly spoke as he looked over the ceiling above. "It never cost him anything to be nice to people. Or something like

37

that," he paraphrased as he returned his vision to his friends who were looking a little forlorn.

"Saito certainly was a wordsmith, huh?" Haru half-smiled.

"Well, he was in a band after all," Daichi casually shrugged.

"Yeah, that makes sense," Matsu chuckled.

"Come on, I don't think Minori would have wanted us to sulk around," Daichi replied, motioning with his head to a train car behind him.

"No…the living shouldn't envy the dead," Minori quietly confirmed, looking up at a train car. "Though a little sulking in private doesn't hurt," he slyly smiled, giving Daichi a wink.

The teens continued to explore all the museum had to offer, which was surprisingly a lot: two connected buildings, four floors, a massive diorama, train cars, plenty of exhibit rooms, and even some beautiful stained-glass windows! If they had thought ahead, there were even some hands-on exhibits, like a theatre, a miniature driving train, and plenty of different simulators they could have partaken in.

"This place is far more impressive than I remembered," Minori commented as they rode the escalator up to the second floor.

"It's a good thing we got here early," Daichi replied.

"Yeah, no kidding!" Matsu beamed.

"We'll be here all day," Haru noted, glancing around as they all ascended above the Rolling Stock Station.

"I don't have any complaints about that," Daichi admitted, resting his hands behind his head.

"Yeah, me neither. Not like I had any other plans today," Matsu agreed.

"Yeah, me neither," Haru smiled.

"This should be a fun-filled day," Minori smiled.

Daichi smiled back in agreement as the group reached the top of the escalator.

"Alright, second floor," Haru noted, being the first to step off the escalator. First living human anyway. "What do you guys want to check out first?"

Daichi looked to Matsu, who was the one who had been charged with the map. Matsu shrugged, not appearing to take the cue.

"Matsuda, you have the map," Daichi explained.

"Oh! Right!" the spiky-haired blond acknowledged before pulling the map out from his back pocket. "Well, to the right, we have the Future Station, and to the left, we have a bunch of other stuff we can see."

"Well, if there's only one room to the right, it would make sense to check that out first," Haru proposed, looking down the pathway to their right.

"Makes sense to me," Daichi agreed.

"Alright, lead the way, Hayashi," Matsu smiled, returning the map to his pocket.

The Future Station, as the name implied, was dedicated to the envisioning of the railways of the future. And rather than a room, it was a stretch of walkway with various freestanding, white numbered structures. To the exhibit's credit, it did instill the feeling of the future. They didn't linger very long, going through the station fairly quickly, Haru leading the charge.

The group briefly checked out the Job Station housed in the same 'building,' per Haru's orders, though like the Future Station, they didn't linger long before they were on their way back to where they had come up from.

"Well, that was informational," Matsu frowned.

"Yeah, not as impressive as the main floor," Haru

agreed as he continued to lead the group. "But that's to be expected."

"Well, there's plenty more to see. We can't write off the museum yet," Daichi smiled.

"I'm sure the other exhibits will be more fun," Minori assured.

"Where to next?" Haru asked, glancing back over his broad shoulders at the rest of the group.

"Let's just keep going this way," Daichi replied.

"Alright then," Haru shrugged as they began passing a historical timeline display.

"I think the diorama is over this way," Matsu said as they approached the end of the walkway.

"That could be cool," Daichi replied.

"Alright, let's check it out," Haru said as the group took a right turn.

They found the diorama room without any trouble. It was right across from the stained-glass windows and a set of stairs.

"This is crazy," Daichi commented as he studied the diorama from behind the railing that separated it from the museum's visitors.

"This certainly beats the Future Station," Minori replied, placing his hand on his chin. He moved closer to the model to get a better view from close up.

"Get–" Daichi instinctively began to chastise him.

"This must have taken forever to build," Matsu interjected.

"I can't even imagine the amount of work that went into this thing," Haru commented from beside him.

"There's so many tiny details," Minori whispered as he moved his head, studying the tiny people and trees on display as he floated above them.

I guess this is the one time being a ghost comes in handy, Daichi mentally noted as he watched Minori float around the diorama, getting up close and personal with it.

"Hey, Daichi!" Minori called from within a cluster of buildings.

Daichi's head snapped up from a section of the diorama he had been studying to see Minori give his best giant monster impression, complete with dinosaur-esque squealing. It wasn't hard to tell which one he was impersonating with his body language, summoning forth a burst of laughter from Daichi, which caught both Haru and Matsu off guard, as well as the handful of other visitors.

"Oh, sorry," Daichi apologized, reining in his laughter.

"What was that all about?" Haru asked, raising an eyebrow.

"I just imagined what it would be like to stand in there pretending to be Gojira," Daichi chuckled.

Haru cracked a smile before looking back at the massive structure beside them. "That would be kind of funny," he admitted.

Daichi could hear Minori let out a subdued roar, which forced a bit of laughter out from him. "Sorry," he apologized again, trying to get himself under control.

"Alright, let's go before Takahashi has another laughing fit," Haru said as he began to make his way out.

"Wait! Just one more!" Minori pleaded, drawing Daichi's gaze again. Minori launched into one more full-body impression, this time complete with his own sound effects, which once again warranted another laugh from Daichi.

"Takahashi," Matsu hissed, grabbing Daichi by the arm and pulling him along as he tried to compose himself.

"I can't help it," Daichi chuckled as he held his sides.

41

"You're unbelievable," Haru muttered.

The next stop on the Haru-led tour was the Railway Cultural Gallery, a small room with a collection of images, music, film, and even food related to the aforementioned subject. It was a visually stimulating enough room; it looked like an art gallery, which Daichi supposed it more or less was. It even had the wood flooring you think of when you think of an art studio. They didn't spend much time in the room, but they all agreed it hadn't been the worst stop on the tour.

"You guys want to get something to eat?" Matsu asked as they exited the gallery.

"I could go for some food," Haru admitted as he peered down at the rest of them, inadvertently reminding them all of his height.

"I think we passed a spot on our way over here," Matsu replied, glancing around.

"Yeah, but that was a restaurant, wasn't it?" Haru asked.

"That's what I thought," Daichi agreed.

"I thought I saw another place," Matsu replied, pulling out the map again from his pocket. "Looks like there's a couple places. If we go up a floor, we could eat at the Shinkansen Lounge."

"Works for me," Haru said.

"Sure, I don't have any problems with that either," Daichi agreed.

"I'd protest, but I don't think anyone would listen," Minori teased.

"Alright, lead the way, Matsuda," Haru said, turning to the side to allow Matsu to lead.

"We should just be able to take the elevator right up to it," Matsu explained, pointing to a nearby elevator.

"Cool," Haru replied, following after Matsu, who had begun making his way.

Just as Matsu said, the lounge was just outside the elevator when they stepped out onto the third floor. It was nice getting to sit down after having spent the past couple hours walking around; it was a good thing they had come as soon as the doors opened because, as Haru had predicted, it had started to get crowded now that it was noon.

"Good call coming as early as possible," Daichi praised as he glanced around.

"Yeah, no kidding," Matsu agreed. "It's only been a couple hours and it's already pretty crowded."

"Well, it is a Sunday," Haru replied. "We might have had better luck if we had gone during the week, but Takahashi insisted on coming today instead of waiting, as I had suggested."

"You won't find me complaining," Matsu grinned. "I can't remember the last time we hung out like this."

"Matsuda, we literally all just went to the City Dome together," Haru rebutted.

"I meant not counting that!" Matsu exclaimed.

"Yeah, I guess we have been a while, huh?" Haru acknowledged, crossing his arms.

"Like I said, I'm not complaining. I guess I'm just surprised is all," Matsu smiled, looking at the others at the table.

"Yeah, don't get me wrong, but what's that about, Takahashi?" Haru asked, almost bluntly.

"Yeah, you're not planning on moving away or something, are you?" Matsu grilled, looking to his right at Daichi.

"Oh, no, it's nothing like that!" Daichi sheepishly assured.

43

"So, what is it, then?" Haru asked, almost appearing surprised? "Like I said, don't take this the wrong way, but I didn't exactly think you viewed us as all that close."

Daichi frowned, "It's just that…" Haru raised an eyebrow as Matsu leaned closer to Daichi.

"Ugh, it's gonna sound stupid," Daichi groaned. "But you guys are really my only friends, you know? It's just, I don't want to wake up one day having wished I had spent more time with you guys is all."

"That makes sense," Matsu replied, looking up at the ceiling.

"Works for me," Haru shrugged before taking a bite of his food.

"Thanks, guys," Daichi smiled as he stared at his lap.

"We'll always be friends, Daichi!" Matsu beamed, grabbing Daichi by the neck with his arm and pulling him close.

"Stop!" Daichi laughed as he pried himself away from the blond ruffian.

"Oh, I know!" Matsu chimed, his eyes suddenly wide.

"What?" Daichi asked, looking at Matsu, puzzled.

Matsu reached up to his right ear and removed his dangling lightning bolt-shaped earring. "Take this," he requested as he held the glossy yellow charm from his fingers.

"But my ears aren't pierced," Daichi replied.

"We could change that," Minori suggested slyly from the chair nearest him.

"So what?" Matsu asked. "That's not the point. I want you to have it as a sign of our friendship."

"Okay then, sure," Daichi obliged slowly, taking the earring from Matsu's hand.

"Well, if that's how it's gonna be," Haru sighed, reaching his hands around the back of his neck and undoing his thin, gold necklace. "Take this," he politely demanded, holding his necklace out across the table to Daichi.

"Whoa, Hayashi, are you sure?" Daichi asked.

"We're friends, right?" Haru asked.

"Well, yeah–" Daichi answered.

"Good, then take it," Haru replied. "Then you'll have something from both of us."

"Alright," Daichi politely said as he took the shimmering piece of gold from his friend. He quickly bent the gold hook of the earring Matsu had given him into a circle.

"What ya' doin'?" Matsu asked, peering over.

"My parents aren't as cool as yours, Matsuda. They're not gonna let me get my ear pierced, but with a little effort, I can make sure both your gifts are always with me," Daichi replied as he fed one end of the necklace through the newly formed loop of the earring.

"Oh, that's a good idea!" Matsu exclaimed.

"I still think I would have preferred the ear-piercing route," Minori teased, resting his chin in his hand as he watched Daichi fasten the necklace.

Daichi rolled his eyes in response.

"Suit yourself," Minori smiled. "I think you'd look dashing with one earring."

"Well, my parents would not," Daichi instinctively replied.

"They wouldn't?" Matsu asked, sounding concerned, reminding Daichi that only he could see and hear Minori.

"Oh, sorry," Daichi sheepishly smiled, "I was thinking out loud."

The group relaxed for a bit longer, enjoying their lunch and having further idle chitchat before they continued on their way.

"While we're up here, do you guys want to check out the Science Station?" Matsu asked as he read over the map.

"We might as well since we're already up here," Haru replied.

"Yeah, for sure," Daichi agreed.

"Then we can pick up where we left off on the second floor and call it a day," Haru suggested, glancing around the busy space.

"Sounds good to me," Daichi smiled.

"Alright, let's mosey!" Matsu chimed, leading the charge.

The Science Station was a hands-on experience. There were several different devices to mess with to show the science behind railways. It was one of the lesser experiences for Daichi, seeing as one member of their group was incapable of experiencing it to its fullest.

"Well, that was depressing," Minori lamented as the teens exited the Science Station.

"Sorry, Minori," Daichi frowned as he walked beside the somber spirit behind his friends. Matsu and Haru both glanced back over their shoulders

"You say something, Daichi?" Matsu asked.

"Oh, sorry, just thinking out loud again," Daichi chuckled, holding up a hand.

"Oh, alright," Matsu replied.

The teens returned to the second floor, only this time opting for the stairs, as they were closer to the exit of the Science Station. It turned out they had only missed two rooms on the second floor, neither being of much merit. They had debated walking to the other side of the museum and back up a floor to see the History Station, but after a full day of walking around, it was apparent to anyone that they were done. Ending their experience on a low note, they decided to make their way to the exit, checking out a couple of train cars they had missed earlier.

"Well, overall, I'd say today was a success," Matsu smiled as they all stood out in front of the museum.

"We definitely could have done worse," Haru agreed.

"I'd say it was about as I remembered, even as a ghost," Minori delightfully smiled.

"Yeah," Daichi nodded. "That was cool."

"So, what do we do now?" Matsu inquired.

"I've got to head home. I've got basketball practice," Haru explained.

"That just leaves you and me, Daichi," Matsu smiled, looking at Daichi.

"I can't either," Daichi sheepishly smiled, holding up his hand.

"Aw, really?" Matsu replied, almost without sounding convinced.

"Yeah, sorry," Daichi apologized. *I don't want to be rude, but I'm all people'd out for the day, plus I really want to get to spend some more alone time with Minori. We've almost beaten Final Fantasy VI; it's not on the bucket list, but I've really enjoyed getting to experience it with him.* "Oh, I did want to ask you guys something, though," Daichi added.

"What's that?" Haru asked.

"What do you guys think about going to the Gion Matsuri?" Daichi proposed.

"That sounds fun!" Matsu eagerly exclaimed.

"We could do that, but the big event days have

already happened. Why don't we go to Tenjin Matsuri instead?" Haru suggested. "It's in just a couple days."

Daichi thought it over for a moment, "Eh, yeah, but if we go to Gion Matsuri, we can also visit the Fushimi Inari Shrine," he frowned.

"Hm, then it would make more sense to go to the Gion Matsuri considering it's all the way over in Kyoto," Haru acknowledged, crossing his arms.

"We could do both," Matsu shrugged.

"I supposed we could," Daichi admitted as he laced his hands behind his head.

"If we plan on doing that, then we'll have to go to Tenjin Matsuri first, since I think it only runs for a couple days," Haru said.

"Sounds good to me," Daichi shrugged.

"I'm down!" Matsu happily proclaimed.

"Alright, sounds like a plan, then," Haru replied. "Tenjin starts in two days, so that's when we'll go. Keep it simple."

"Okay," Daichi agreed.

"How exciting! Not one but two festivals?" Minori smiled. "Daichi, you spoil me."

"Whatever," Daichi chuckled, glancing at the corporeal boy to his right who was doing a small dance.

"Do you not like that idea?" Haru asked, appearing a little taken aback.

Dammit, I did it again! Daichi internally screamed as his stomach sank. "No, sorry! I was just–" Daichi replied, fumbling his words.

"Talking to yourself again?" Matsu asked.

"You know, Takahashi, talking to yourself is a sign of loneliness," Haru bluntly explained.

"I'm not lonely!" Daichi retorted. "I just think out loud sometimes!"

"Whatever you say," Haru replied.

"So, what's the plan? We all meet up at Takahashi's house before heading to the festival?" Matsu asked for clarification.

"Works for me," Haru agreed.

"Yeah, that works," Daichi huffed.

And like that, once again, our list grew by one.....

Daichi and I spent the next two days alone playing Final Fantasy VI.

I had never really played an RPG before. I don't think I would have the patience to do it on my own, let alone the time.

But I found the experience really enjoyable. But maybe that was because I was merely an observer. Daichi had certainly become frustrated with the whole ordeal more than once…

Who would have thought such a plain old thing as playing video games with someone could be so memorable?

On another note.

I must say, even though we spent the Tenjin Matsuri with his friends, I found it really fun. (My compliments to Hayashi for the suggestion.) It made me happy to see Daichi having so much fun. We even got to sit and watch fireworks together! They were so stunning. It was so magical that for a moment, I had forgotten I was dead.

Watching the beautiful explosions of color with Daichi beside me…If I had a heart, it would have been racing, for sure.

I only wished I could have experienced the festival with him while I was alive…

And while I did have a wonderful time with him and his friends, I did make one request after the festival....

I wanted him to invite some of my friends to the next one, even if they'd say no....

STAGE 4:

ANGER

*I find anger is a fickle mistress; she seems to come and go
on a whim.*

*I had thought after all this time that had passed, I had
gotten over being angry about being dead.*

But turns out, I hadn't…

I just found new reasons to be angry.

*Originally, I was just mad because of course I was.When
the world around you continues to move forward without
you and all you can do is watch…
You feel…*

*Powerless.
Insignificant.*

*Which of course, sure, in the grand scheme of things,
humans are.
But…
I don't think most of us notice that while we're alive.
I certainly didn't....*

*But after I died, rather than being an actor on a stage, I
was just an audience member.
A mute audience member, and no matter how much noise
I tried to make,
Nobody could hear me....*

Until Daichi.

*And for the first time in what had felt like a lifetime, I–Well,
you can imagine, I felt alive again, myself again.*

I didn't find myself angry at the Gion Matsuri because the world had continued to move without me. I was angry because…it had given me a taste of what my future could have been, full well knowing it was no longer within my reach and never would be, no matter how much I screamed.

No matter how much I begged.

Pleaded.

Or.

Fought.

I was dead.
And my future was null and void.

No matter what....

"You okay, Minori?" Daichi asked as he approached the semi-translucent boy floating beside a bench that was askew. They had broken off from the rest of their friends to enjoy the Fushimi Inari Shrine, just the two of them.

"I'm okay," Minori replied as he gazed out at the city lights in the distance.

Visiting the shrine the same day as the festival had worked out great; the shrine had only been about a thirty-minute train ride away from the Kyoto City Center, where the festival was being held. The day had started out great. They had boarded the train back home in Saitama early in the day, dressed in their best yukata, and ridden it all the way to Kyoto, but as the day had gone on, Minori had grown…distant. He seemed upset, but he wouldn't say anything when Daichi asked.

"Are you sure you're alright?" Daichi asked, sitting down on the metal bench, next to Minori. "You seem upset."

Minori sighed, appearing to want to talk, while simultaneously struggling to allow his walls to come down.

"I can understand if you don't want to," Daichi added. "I'm not exactly an expert on opening up to people either. I guess I just want you to know I'm here; you don't have to bear the burden of silence."

"When did you get so wise?" Minori warily smiled.

"I like to think I had a good teacher," Daichi fondly replied. "You, you're the teacher, in case you didn't get that."

Minori smiled. *Finally, a smile,* Daichi internally exhaled. *I was starting to get worried that there'd be no saving this date. Wait, is this a date? No, that'd be weird! Right?* He quietly argued with himself as he studied Minori's androgynous face.

"I guess…" Minori started to speak. "Ugh, forget it,

it's–it's dumb."

"If it's upsetting you, it's not dumb," Daichi assured.

"I'm sorry," Minori sheepishly replied, running his hand through his hair and scratching the back of his head. "I've always been terrible at expressing how I feel."

"Huh," Daichi replied, a little surprised. He would have thought the opposite, seeing how Minori had been a musician–a singer, no less. "I never would have guessed," he quickly expounded.

"It's just–when I try to speak about how I'm feeling when I'm upset, it's like my emotions override my words and stop them from coming out," Minori explained. "It's just like every fiber of my being screams out for me to stop. It makes me want to…want to…just cease existing, I guess."

"Yeah, I suppose if I felt that way when trying to express how I was feeling, I wouldn't want to do it either. That being said, I definitely say things that immediately make me feel embarrassed, especially when I'm talking to you, Minori." Daichi admitted, letting out a nervous laugh. *What the Hell? Why would you say that? He's going to think you're weird! What guy says that to another guy?* Daichi silently chastised so loudly inside his head, he almost found it surprising Minori couldn't hear him.

"Well, if that's how you feel," Minori fondly smiled, closing his eyes, "I suppose it's only fair I express how I feel then as well."

"Y-You don't have to!" Daichi stammered. "I'd hate to put you in an uncomfortable situation!"

"Well, from the sounds of it, I do it a lot to you, so fair is fair," Minori smiled, looking Daichi's way.

"I didn't mean it like that!" Daichi exclaimed.

Minori groaned, raking his hand through his hair. "It's just, I've had so much fun," he explained as he averted his eyes from Daichi. "And it just made me frustrated, I guess, because I wish–I wish we could have hung out like this when I was alive."

"That makes sense," Daichi replied, looking up at the pale, beautiful boy hovering near him. "I wish we could have, too, trust me, but–but at least we are now, you know? It's not ideal, but I'll take us being able to now than never having done it at all."

"I know you're right," Minori sighed, rubbing the back of his neck, visibly uncomfortable. "Still doesn't mean it doesn't suck."

Daichi completely understood he would never admit it to anyone, but he definitely had imagined what it would have been like to experience the festivals together while Minori was alive, walking hand in hand, looking at all the stalls, buying each other gifts. He briefly thought of what Minori's yukata would have looked like. Something flowery, he bet.

"It's just not fair," Minori muttered, looking away.

"I don't think anyone would say what happened to you was fair, Minori," Daichi mumbled in agreement. "If the roles were reversed, I'd be mad, too."

"Ugh, I'm sorry!" Minori groaned, his eyes tightly pulling shut as he rubbed the back of his neck. "I ruined our day out together."

"What?" Daichi shouted. "Not at all! No one would expect you to be cheery all the time!"

"Still," Minori frowned, looking away, "you planned this lovely day for us, and I've been moping around for half of it. It's not fair to you."

"Well, I guess you'll just have to make it up to me," Daichi smiled, standing up. "We've still got time before we head home, so why don't we check out more of the shrine together?"

"I'd love that," Minori apologetically smiled.

"Alright then, let's go," Daichi replied with a smile still plastered to his face.

"Lead the way." Minori gracefully bowed like a proper gentleman; it made Daichi feel a way he wasn't accustomed to, but he wasn't mad about it. Minori was always making him feel this way. Special? Was that the word? It was hard for him to understand. "Something the matter?" Minori asked, peering up from his bow.

"Sorry!" Daichi exclaimed, coming to his senses and taking the lead. *Stupid! What was that all about? You can't just be staring at another man!* he mentally admonished as he walked away from the cliff face.

The shrine was pretty busy this evening, which wasn't surprising with it being near the festival, coupled with the fact that it was a bit of a tourist hotspot; there were plenty of foreigners and locals alike, but that didn't stop Daichi from talking out loud to Minori. He had gotten over the fact that it made him look like a weirdo. It wasn't like he was ever going to see any of these people again anyway. It was hardly much of a price to pay to help Minori feel like a person again. If it made him happy, it was worth it.

The shrine was of considerable size, so they had plenty left to see before returning to the entrance to meet up with the rest of their group.

"There he is!" Matsu chimed as Daichi walked down the stone steps of the shrine to rejoin his friends.

"We had thought you might have gotten lost," Haru said, placing his hands in the sleeves of his yukata.

"I was just taking my time," Daichi smiled, chuckling slightly.

"Did you make sure to pay your respects?" Kurashita inquired.

"Yeah, of course I did," Daichi replied, kind of surprised she'd even ask, but then again, it wasn't like they really knew each other very well. Outside their mutual

61

friendship with Minori and Matsu, they didn't really know each other; he was kind of surprised she had agreed to go with them.

"Well, if we're all done here, let's get heading home. It's a long train ride back to Saitama," Nakamura said as he stood apart from the group with his hands in his pockets, the only one in the group not dressed in traditional attire.

"Yeah, the last train leaves in an hour, so we really should get going so we don't miss it," Kutchek agreed.

"Can you imagine if we got stuck here?" Matsu beamed.

"There are worse places to be trapped," Minori smiled as he floated beside Daichi.

"I'd rather not," Haru replied.

"Yeah, me neither, so let's go!" Nakamura motioned away from the shrine with his head.

"So impatient," Kurashita sighed.

"He always has been," Kutchek chuckled.

"Whatever," Nakamura muttered as he began to leave, but he quickly stopped to spin around and bow, paying one last respect to Inari before walking away. The rest of the group did the same and followed behind, Kutchek jogging to catch up to his brother.

"Saito would have liked this," Kurashita smiled as she walked beside Daichi, watching Kutchek heckle his tall, dark, and gloomy sibling.

"I'm sure he would have," Daichi agreed.

"All things considered, yes, yes, I did," Minori smiled, not walking beside Daichi but instead beside Kurashita.

"I know he doesn't show it, but Nakamura needed this," Kurashita mumbled. "He's been taking Saito's death pretty hard. He doesn't show it, but Kutchek told me he can tell."

"I guess that makes sense. They were in a band together, after all; I'm sure they were close," Daichi replied, looking past Kurashita to Minori.

"Oda was my best friend," Minori frowned, looking straight ahead at Nakamura in the distance. "I tried to reach him, I really did, but…no matter how hard I tried, I couldn't."

"I'm sure Nakamura was Minori's best friend, too," Daichi said, more or less relaying Minori's message.

"Yeah, the two were inseparable," Kurashita fondly smiled.

"Yeah, even I could see that," Daichi agreed. "Nakamura always seemed to be hanging off Minori."

"But you guys were close, too, right?" Kurashita asked.

"Yeah, I guess you could say that," Daichi smiled, not sure how to respond.

"How are you holding up? I didn't even think to ask the last time we spoke," Kurashita asked.

"I'm okay," Daichi replied. "Apparently doing better than Nakamura is."

"Good to hear," Kurashita warmly smiled.

"To be honest, I'm surprised he came along," Daichi admitted.

"I think he was just looking for a reason to leave the house," Kurashita replied.

"So I guess that means the band isn't meeting up right now," Daichi inferred.

"No, it's just too soon for them, I think," Kurashita frowned. "They all need time to process everything."

"That's fair," Daichi replied. *I suppose it's probably too soon to tell him Minori would want them to continue on,* he quietly contemplated as he watched the long-haired youth walk beside the much shorter, ginger-haired boy. "Kutchek is Nakamura's brother, right? How does that work?"

"Kutchek's mother moved here from America when he was just a kid. I guess she met Nakamura's dad, and before you knew it, they were married," Kurashita explained.

"That makes sense," Daichi replied. "I was surprised when he said his brother would be coming along and Kutchek showed up. I've seen him around school, but I had no idea he was Nakamura's brother."

"Surprised me the first time, too!" Minori exclaimed with a laugh. "You should have seen the look on my face the first time I went over to Oda's house. I bet I looked so silly!"

"Were Kutchek and Minori close?" Daichi asked again, looking past Kurashita for the answer.

"No more than you and I were before I died," Minori casually replied. "We always got along just fine, and sure, we hung out occasionally with one another as a part of a group, but that's about it."

"I see," Daichi replied, completely ignoring whatever answer Kurashita had given.

"He mainly hangs out with the foreign exchange students," Kurashita said, grabbing Daichi's attention.

"That sounds about right," Minori corroborated.

"I suppose that makes sense, him being a foreigner and all," Daichi replied.

"Though he certainly doesn't act it," Kurashita giggled.

"Of course he doesn't," Haru said from behind, catching them both off guard.

"Have you been listening this whole time?" Daichi asked.

"Well, you guys are walking right in front of us," Matsu politely argued.

"Kutchek was raised here, from the sounds of it, so

as far as I'm concerned, he's just as Japanese as the rest of us, even if he doesn't look it," Haru said, sounding disappointed. "It's not right to assume he should act a certain way solely because he wasn't born here or doesn't look like the rest of us."

"I don't think Kurashita meant any offense," Daichi meekly replied.

"It doesn't matter. It may not seem offensive to us, but if you were to say something like that to Kutchek, he may think differently. Like I said, once you put aside the color of his skin and the origin of his birth, he's really not all that different from us. He's a Japanese citizen. He's one of us, not an animal on display for our amusement," Haru coldly retorted.

"Whoa," Matsu breathed.

"Yeah, that was a little harsh, don't you think?" Daichi asked.

"Let me ask you something," Haru retorted, stopping in place, forcing the others to stop with him. "If I told you I was only half Japanese, would that change how you view my actions?"

"No, of course not," Daichi replied, surprised he would even ask.

"Then you shouldn't look at Kutchek any differently either just because he's white, or not originally from here," Haru explained.

"When you put it that way," Daichi frowned.

"I guess we owe Kutchek an apology," Kurashita replied, glancing at Daichi.

"Yeah, I guess we do," Daichi agreed. "Thanks for putting it in perspective, Hayashi."

"Anytime," Haru replied, placing a strong hand on Daichi's shoulder. "That's what friends are for."

"Hey, Kutchek," Daichi said as he and Kurashita approached the boy outside the train station.

"What's up?" Kutchek asked, turning to face the two.

"We wanted to apologize," Daichi replied.

"Okay…for what?" Kutchek asked, clearly not sure why they were apologizing.

"We really misjudged you because you were a foreigner, and it wasn't fair," Kurashita quickly blurted out as she went into a deep bow.

"We shouldn't have assumed just because you're not from here that you would act like every other foreigner who just comes to visit!" Daichi quickly added, he, too, ducking into a deep bow.

"Well, I guess that makes sense," Kutchek casually replied.

"Huh?" Daichi and Kurashita simultaneously replied, both clearly surprised.

"To be fair, if the situation was reversed, I would have probably thought the same thing, honestly," Kutchek replied.

"Please, forgive us," Daichi politely requested.

"It's okay," Kutchek smiled, patting Daichi on the head and then Kurashita. "I forgive you guys."

"You guys are lucky he isn't me," Nakamura said from behind his brother a few feet away. "I would have told you both to go to Hell."

"Nobody is perfect," Kutchek shrugged, looking back at his brother with a warm smile.

"Let's go. The train is leaving soon," Nakamura replied, continuing on his way to the train platform.

"You think Nakamura will forgive us?" Daichi asked as he straightened up.

"He'll be fine," Kutchek replied with a wave of his hand, making it look like the flipper of a penguin. "He's just dealing with a lot right now, so all of his emotions are, like, set to ten, except for happiness, obviously."

"Come on, let's hurry up," Haru said, placing his hands on Kurashita and Daichi's shoulders.

"Yeah, we don't want to miss the train," Kutchek agreed. "Oh, by the way, you guys can just call me Rory. All my other friends do."

With the evening ending on an important lesson…
We struck two more things from the bucket list.

The only thing left to do now was take a trip across the country.

Which wasn't going to be easy…

But Daichi was confident he could pull it off…

Despite having all the time in the world, it felt like we were on a time crunch, which I suppose we technically were. We had a month left of summer break, which sure was a good amount of time on its own, but Hokkaido was a full day's trip by car, and who knew if we could even pull something like that off....

And yet somehow....

Once again, my knight in shining armor came through and led me on the adventure of a lifetime

STAGE 5:

ACCEPTANCE

"You want to take a road trip…to Hokkaido?" Nakamura asked, sitting across from Daichi with his arms crossed in front of his chest.

"I know it sounds crazy, but it's important!" Daichi replied.

"What's so important that you'd go out of your way to rope me into this?" Nakamura asked, leaning back in his seat.

"Minori," Daichi mumbled, looking at the fast-food table in front of him. "It was one of things he wanted to do before he died."

"Did he really say that?" Nakamura asked as he gazed up at the ceiling.

"Yeah," Daichi quietly replied. "You were his best friend, but I barely knew him, and I just—I don't know. I want—I want to do this for him; he was always so kind to me, you know? I want to honor him."

"Daichi, you flatter me," Minori teased as he leaned across the table, looking like an incubus.

"Hmmm," Nakamura thought for a moment, closing his eyes. "Traveling across Japan would be pretty rad; that was always the dream anyway, right?"

"Yeah, it was," Minori fondly smiled, his eyes fixed on the table.

"We were going to tour all over Japan. He always used to say," Nakamura began, his words cut off by his laughter, "'Mark my words, Oda, one day, we're going to tour the world!' You should have seen him, man; he was always such, like, a dandy, you know? But when he got on stage, that's when he'd come alive. He was like a different person."

"I bet," Daichi replied, politely listening to all Nakamura had to say.

The raven-haired teenager across from him fell silent, allowing the quiet goings-on of the restaurant to fill the void left in the air.

Nakamura let out a heavy sigh as he hung his head. "Man, I really miss him," he mumbled.

"Yeah, me too," Daichi softly agreed. "That's why I want to take this trip."

"So why not do it by yourself?" Nakamura asked.

"Because…I think Minori would want all his friends to do it together," Daichi explained.

"Absolutely," Minori warmly smiled as he drew circles on the table with his finger.

"I see," Nakamura mumbled. And once again, the silence took hold. "Come on, Oda, think about it. We could see all the places we talked about," Minori smiled, his eyes still fixed on the table. "There's a big world out there to see."

"So, how do you intend to do it?" Nakamura asked, resting his chin in his hand as he looked out the window beside them.

"So you'll come?" Minori exclaimed as he snapped upright, looking at Nakamura with exuberant eyes.

"So you'll do it?" Daichi eagerly asked.

"It was Minori's wish, right?" Nakamura nonchalantly asked as his dark eyes studied the world outside. "I'd hate to disappoint his spirit or whatever. He'd probably haunt me from beyond the grave if I said no."

"I had considered it," Minori slyly smiled, looking Nakamura's way.

"Yeah, he probably would do something petty like that, huh?" Daichi said with a laugh.

"Now wait just a minute, mister!" Minori retorted.

"You have no idea," Nakamura smiled. He smiled! Daichi wasn't sure he was capable of such a thing, especially after what Rory had told them. "He could be pretty petty when he wanted to be; the guy was a bit of a diva."

"Oh, was he?" Daichi smirked, looking at Minori.

"I was no such thing!" Minori replied. "I just know what I want is all!"

"Oh, yeah," Nakamura said, still looking out the window. "There were a couple times he had been petty to other bands who had offended him."

"Oh, really?" Daichi asked with a smile fixed on his face.

"Hey, those bands deserved it," Minori pouted as he crossed his arms and looked away.

"Yeah, Minori was a great guy, but you never wanted to get on his bad side," Nakamura explained. "I remember, once, he was so mad at all of us, he gave us the silent treatment all the way until our performance."

"Sounds kind of childish," Daichi chuckled.

"It happens," Nakamura replied with a smile still on his face. "We were all the best of friends; when you're in a band, it's just different. You fight, you cry, you take the highs and the lows with each other. You're a family."

"That makes sense," Daichi replied.

"No relationship is perfect," Nakamura said. "No exceptions."

"I know what you mean," Daichi quietly replied.

"So, you never answered my question," Nakamura reminded, his eyes shifting to Daichi. "How do you intend to pull this off?"

"Well, I still have some money saved up from part-time work, so I figured if everyone pitched in, it should be enough to afford the trip," Daichi explained.

"That makes sense," Nakamura replied. "I'll ask the other guys if they'll come with, then."

"So, the next problem will just be finding someone who can rent a car," Daichi said as he thought it over.

"Don't worry about that," Nakamura replied, sitting back in his seat. "The band has a van. As long as I can convince Makoto to come with, it shouldn't be a problem."

"You guys have a van?" Daichi exclaimed. Minori had never mentioned this! Then again, Daichi did suppose it had never come up in their conversations. Maybe that was part of the reason Minori asked Daichi to invite his friends along.

"Well, yeah, what kind of band would we be if we didn't?" Nakamura asked. "Makoto is the only one of us who can drive, though, so I'm really going to have to sell him on the idea."

"Do you think he'll agree to come along?" Daichi asked.

"Makoto is pretty frugal, but I think if I tell him it's for Minori, he'll agree to do it," Nakamura replied. "I'll reach out to the other guys and get back to you," he added as he got out of the plastic booth, passing right through Minori.

"Okay, great! Talk to you later!" Daichi beamed.

"Later," Nakamura shortly replied as he walked around the booth.

And so, we waited....

If I'm being honest, I fully expected them all to have said no.

But like true friends, they all said yes.

The last step was to get Daichi's mother to agree to let him drive across the country with a bunch of rowdy boys she didn't even know, ha, ha, ha.

Q.F.I. wasn't exactly known as a mellow band, ha, ha, ha, which I'm sure my on-stage antics are partially to blame for. But people paid for a show, not a night at the opera....wait, maybe that's not quite a good analogy…

I suppose I sell Daichi's salesman skills too short because it really didn't take much convincing to get his family on board. One heartfelt speech and a few days later, his parents agreed to let us go.

With the stipulation that he needed to check in twice a day, but a small price to pay, if you ask me.

And so we were off. We left August 1 at nine a.m.

栃木県

TOCHIGI

The first prefecture we passed through on our trip was home to many a wondrous sight, one of them being Mt. Nantai, which was nearby Nikkō Tōshō-gū, a shrine dedicated to the first shogun military leader. Seeing as we were on a pilgrimage of sorts, we felt it was only right to stop by the shrine and pay our respects. Besides, it wasn't like it was that far off the beaten trail, and what good is a road trip if you're not going to explore? And since the shrine was so close to Mt. Nantai and Lake Chūzenji, I thought it'd be a shame if we skipped out on seeing them. Luckily, Makoto agreed with Daichi and I, so we visited those as well, but Kegon Falls was on the way, so it wasn't like we could skip out on that either!

"I wouldn't have guessed we would have to take an elevator to see the falls," Yuuki chimed as the teens all rode their way up to the outside viewing area for the falls.

"Yeah, me either," Daichi beamed. "Kind of cool, huh?"

"Speak for yourselves," Makoto warily replied, gripping the railing of the steel box they stood in. Daichi looked back at the heavier-set boy with a sort of buzz cut and black, thick-rimmed glasses. "Makoto, are you afraid of elevators?" he chuckled.

"Shut up, dude!" Makoto replied as he stared up at the ceiling. "You guys are all skinny! You don't have to worry about being too heavy!"

"Makoto, you do realize the elevator is rated for, like, thousands of pounds right?" Nakamura asked, appearing exasperated.

"Dude, whatever. Doesn't mean it doesn't freak me out!" Makoto shouted.

"Well, we're almost to the top," Daichi smiled as Minori fought back his laughter.

"*If* we make it to the top," Makoto replied just as the box shook. Makoto let out a banshee scream as he frantically looked to his friends, the shaking subsiding just as quickly as it appeared, the elevator coming to a complete stop.

"See, we made it," Nakamura replied as he made his way out of the dirty-looking white box of metal. Minori in full laughter as he followed behind his friend.

"Just give me a second," Makoto breathed as Yuuki tried to pull him along by the sleeve of his black hooded sweatshirt.

Daichi left Yuuki to deal with Makoto as he and the bassist for the band, Kotarō, exited the elevator.

They joined the other two at the railing facing the falls; Nakamura rested his back against the rail, his hands in the pockets of his jeans. "Behold, Kegon Falls," he apathetically greeted as they closed the distance between them.

"Wow," Kotarō breathed.

"Somehow, I wasn't expecting this," Daichi said as he joined Minori off to the side, near some mounted binoculars.

"It's beautiful, isn't it?" Minori asked as he dreamily

gazed at the roaring water.

"It's sure something," Daichi admitted, leaning against the hot metal rail. *Who would have thought this was where I'd end up a few months ago?* he quietly mused to himself as he studied the giant falls in the distance. *Certainly not me, yet here I am with the ghost of Minori Saito, and I've literally never been happier than I am right now, and I don't even know half the people I'm here with. And yet here we are, all together, bonded by one amazing person.*

Daichi glanced at Minori on his right, who was lovingly beholding the falls. *I like seeing him like this, so at peace, even if it does make me a little sad. I just wish I could have seen him like this when he was still alive,* Daichi noted as he studied his friend, who paid him no mind. *I wonder, though...if Minori had never died, would we—would we have even ever become this close?* Daichi asked himself before returning his gaze to the falls. *Probably not. Minori is way out of my league—I mean as a friend! He's, like, way too cool to waste his time hanging out with someone as average as me,* Daichi continued to monologue, his eyes drifting back to Minori.

"Great place for a date, huh?" he slyly asked, catching Daichi's gaze.

"W-W-What?" Daichi stammered, tripping over his words; he could feel his face heating up. Minori simply smiled with his chin in his hand. He motioned with his head for Daichi to look behind him. Daichi looked back over his shoulder to see a couple not much older than them, the girlfriend forcing her boyfriend to take selfies with her. "Oh, yeah, I suppose it is," Daichi mumbled, watching the two. "They must really be in love."

"Sure appears so," Minori replied, his voice so soft— so seductive—Daichi couldn't help but turn back around to face him. "Have you ever been in love before, Daichi?"

"Me?" Daichi asked, a little caught off guard.

Minori chuckled, "Well, there isn't another Daichi here, is there?"

"No, I can't say I have," Daichi smiled, looking back at the waterfall. *I like how he says my name...Has it always sounded so nice? Wait, that's weird, dude. Ugh, need to stop thinking stuff like that,* Daichi chastised. "What about you, Minori? You were always really popular with the girls at our school."

"You think so?" Minori asked, sounding more amused than Daichi thought appropriate.

"No, I can't say I've ever been in love. Well, not with someone, anyway. Crushes, sure. But I've never been in love," Minori fondly smiled, looking at the scenery.

"Oh? So there was a girl you liked, then," Daichi concluded, looking at his friend for details. "What was her name?"

Minori laughed. "Well, for starters, they were a he, and second, a gentleman never kisses and tells, my dear Daichi," he smiled.

"Wait–Hold on–Minori," Daichi replied, trying to process what he had just said. "You're gay?"

"Yeah," Minori shrugged.

Daichi just stood flabbergasted for a moment, his mouth agape. He had no idea, none whatsoever. Sure, Minori was a little flamboyant, but he was a performer! He had never thought that Minori was gay! Girls were always talking to him and following him around at school!

"I hope you don't think any less of me," Minori quietly replied as he looked back at the waterfall. "You're actually the first person I've ever told this to."

"I'm...the first?" Daichi whispered, still trying to process this new information. *He's really never told anyone this before?*

"I've wanted to tell you for a while now. It was a...

Let's call it a secret bucket list item, and since this trip might be the last thing we do together, I just wanted to let you know," Minori softly replied.

"So this whole time?" Daichi asked.

"Yeah," Minori warily replied, his eyes now looking down.

"I never would have guessed," Daichi replied, looking back out at the sea of green separated by water. "You were always surrounded by girls, so the idea never even crossed my mind. How long have you–Did you always know?"

"No, not always. Probably around middle school," Minori replied.

"Um, what was it like?" Daichi asked. "Like, how did you know, you know?"

"Hard to say. I suppose during middle school, I was pretty confused. I guess I didn't really *know* until high school," Minori explained. "I suppose it's just like you being a straight person. I just started to take notice of the boys around me. You start finding people cute. Maybe you start staring a little too much at the ones you fancy. Your heart races when the boy you like starts talking to you or calls your name. I think the bigger issue is allowing yourself to experience and accept those feelings. At first, I just thought maybe I was being weird, like I just thought they were really cool, you know? But once I got into high school, it was different. I realized that I didn't just think these boys were cool; I was attracted to them. I don't know if that makes any sense," Minori finished with a shy laugh.

"I think it does," Daichi said, thinking it over. *Am I?* He looked at the pale figure beside him.

"I hope you'll still be my friend, Daichi," Minori smiled, looking back at him, sending Daichi's heart racing.

"Of course you're still my friend!" Daichi exclaimed maybe a little too loudly.

"Hey, Daichi, you okay?" Makoto called from behind him, causing Daichi to flinch.

"Sorry!" Daichi shouted back. *I know being gay is supposed to be wrong, but...knowing Minori is gay...that... that doesn't change anything. He's still Minori. He's still dead. How is it fair he had to keep how he felt a secret from everyone till now? That's–That's not right. He deserved to confess his feelings to his crush, just like anyone else!* Daichi screamed internally as a knot welled up in his throat and his eyes began to water. *Dammit, now I'm crying like an idiot! Pull it together! Minori just confided in you! This is about him, not you!*

"You okay, Daichi?" Minori asked, leaning in closer.

"I'm fine," Daichi sniffed before giving his whole body a shake as if he were trying to expel bad energy from his chakras. "So you said you had crushes before," Daichi smiled, leaning against the railing. "Tell me about them."

"You want to hear about my crushes?" Minori asked, sounding shocked.

"Of course I do," Daichi grinned, looking over at the dapperly dressed ghost. "I'd imagine you haven't had the chance to talk about them before, right?"

"No, I guess not." Minori half-smiled before returning his gaze to the horizon. "Well, there's been a couple. Are there any in particular you want to hear about?"

"What about the most recent one?" Daichi smiled, looking at the pale blue sky as the clouds soared overhead. "What was he like? Do I know him?"

"He's...sweet," Minori replied. "But I don't think he ever noticed me."

"Really?" Daichi politely asked.

"No," Minori chuckled. "I had always hoped we'd get closer one day, and then maybe if I was lucky–Well, I suppose it's pointless now."

85

"What? No way!" Daichi retorted, glaring at Minori. "I'll tell him for you!"

"That's quite alright," Minori chuckled, holding up his hands.

"What's his name? I'll make sure he knows how you felt," Daichi replied, determination burning in his eyes. *I don't know why, but I almost don't want to know who it is,* he quietly noted. *But if it would help Minori, I'll tell whoever it is, wherever they are, his feelings.*

"It's quite alright," Minori protested.

"But, Minori, they'll never know how much they meant to you. Are you really okay with that?" Daichi asked.

"Yeah, it's okay," Minori quietly replied, glancing away. "Besides, it's not like the two of us could have a future now anyway."

"But still," Daichi replied.

"Thank you, Daichi," Minori smiled, looking into Daichi's eyes. *What color were Minori's eyes originally?* Daichi couldn't recall. They just looked blue now, but what had they been before? A warm amber? A beautiful topaz? "You never said if you had been in love," Minori pointed out.

"Me?" Daichi quizzically asked.

"I'm sure with those beautiful emerald eyes of yours, you had plenty of ladies after you," Minori teased.

"No way," Daichi replied, his heart racing like a bullet train. *Why am I getting so worked up?* he silently inquired.

"So, no crushes, then?" Minori slyly smiled.

"To be honest, no," Daichi shrugged. "I guess I've never met anyone that has made me feel the way you described." *Except...Minori kind of makes me feel that way. Naw, it's just a coincidence. He's just a really cool guy I aspire to be like is all. It only makes sense he'd be captivating or whatever.*

"Hey, Daichi!" Yuuki called, grabbing the brown-haired youth's attention. Daichi turned back to face the others who stood at the other end of the lookout. "Come take a picture with us!"

"Duty calls," Minori said, floating past. "Come along, Daichi. We don't want to keep your adoring public waiting."

"Oh, whatever," Daichi chuckled, following behind his friend.

It was such a relief finally coming out to Daichi....

Coming out to anyone, really. It was like...dark energy had been expelled from me.

Like a looming shadow had been vanquished.

Like this gnawing in the back of mind just…went away....

As planned, after Kegon Falls, we went and checked out Mt. Nantai and Lake Chūzenji before turning around and finally visiting Nikkō Tōshō-gū, where we all paid our respects and, of course, Yuuki took more pictures.

And after that, it was time to find a place to stay the night. Luckily for us, Makoto being eighteen allowed us to rent a hotel for the evening. He really was crucial to our whole journey, ha, ha, ha. It had been such a long time since I had a sleepover with anyone other than Daichi. I had forgotten what it was like!

Even though Daichi and I couldn't freely talk to one another, it was nice just to see the guys all together again.

A couple times, I had even forgotten that I was no longer a part of their world.

It was incredible…Despite all odds, here we were, all my favorite people in the world crammed inside a little hotel right beside Lake Chūzenji. If the trees weren't so tall, we could have probably seen the lake from our room, ha, ha, ha.

Tochigi had so much to offer, it was a shame we really could only afford to stay a day. From what Makoto had found on the internet, there was plenty more to see. But we had a schedule to keep and a destination to reach, so we got up early the next morning—despite having stayed up late the night before—ate a lovely breakfast—well, they ate a lovely breakfast—took one last look at Lake Chūzenji, and headed on our way to our next destination.

福島県

FUKUSHIMA

The second stop on our journey to Hokkaido, Fukushima was rather large. Then again, most prefectures are, so we decided to stop in the capital city, aptly named Fukushima City, so as to not stray off the planned route too much. It was a shame it hadn't been cherry blossom season, because according to the internet, Hanamiyama Park is a great place to view them.

It had only taken about three and a half hours to reach Fukushima City from Lake Chūzenji, so we had plenty of time left in the day to explore.

The city was so densely packed with schools, we made a game of it, ha, ha, ha. The idea was to be the first to spot a school. Obviously, Makoto and Kotarō being in the front seat gave them a bit of an advantage; then again, Makoto being preoccupied with driving didn't really leave him the luxury of being involved in the game, as the one who spotted a school first was allowed to punch another passenger in the arm. Barbaric, I know! But you know what they say, "Boys will be boys." Given my current state, I got to merely enjoy the ensuing chaos of a bunch of teenage boys constantly shouting 'school' and punching each other in the arm. Poor Yuuki was definitely on the receiving end the most out of the group. Everyone was just thankful Makoto was really only playing in spirit, as nobody wanted to be hit by one of his punches. He was teamed up with Yuuki, though, so if he were to call out a school, the task of punching someone fell to Yuuki. Hey, if you were going to be punched by someone, Yuuki was probably the guy you'd most want to take a hit from, given his stature.

Fukushima was so densely populated, it was kind of overwhelming, though admittedly, after yesterday, I don't think any of us were recharged enough for another adventure. That being said, the rousing game of punchies definitely was giving everyone the itch to get out of the van and stretch their legs.

Since Makoto was busy driving, the duty of finding somewhere to stop and explore fell upon Yuuki. While I applaud his effort of picking Abukuma Water Park because the name invokes the idea of a good time, Abukuma isn't really a 'water park.' It's more like a barren landscape nestled beside Abukuma River that's seen better days, where an exorbitant amount of ducks like to gather.

But at least we got to stretch our legs, and very serendipitously, we also managed to find a shrine to pay our respects at, making us two for two—well, three for two. There were actually two different shrines at the park Daichi and I visited, so we were actually three for two. Now that I think about it, the park wasn't actually a bad call in hindsight. There were benches to sit and hang out on. Even if there wasn't much to see, it was still nice....

While we were enjoying the outdoors, Makoto took back his duties as 'activities coordinator' and picked our next stop.

Leave it to Makoto to find something for everyone to do. He found a bowling alley not too far away, so after we all had a good stretch and some fresh air, we got back

91

on the road and headed there.

I had never been to a bowling alley before. Actually, most of us hadn't, but Kotarō used to go all the time when he was a kid, so he gave us a rundown of how to play.
Do you 'play' bowling?
It wasn't complicated, so everyone more or less had the basics down by the end of our time there.
It was a nice place—nothing flashy—just a couple 'lanes,' as Kotarō called them, a few different UFO grabber machines, and even a couple of those taiko drum arcade games, which Makoto of course, being our drummer, had to play a couple times before we left, fully trouncing any who opposed him.
The bowling alley even had some ping pong tables set up, so of course we had to play some rounds. Yuuki was easily the best of us all. Even when I was alive, I was no good at ping pong, ha, ha, ha.
It's funny how you can have spent years with people and still learn things you never knew about them.

Before leaving, Yuuki made sure to take a selfie with everyone in front of a very convincing fake panda they had set out in a glass case. After everything was said and done, it was dinnertime, so we drove up the road and ate at a Western-style restaurant where the guys ate pizza.
It had been a while since I missed eating food, but I'd be lying if I said I hadn't been missing it in that moment, not necessarily because I missed the actual act of eating, or even the taste; I missed the table conversations you have with people while sharing a meal. Sure, I had sat through plenty of meals with Daichi, but this was different because everyone was having so much fun. And once again, I was relegated to being an observer. But it was a

small price to pay to spend time with my friends, my band, one last time....

93

宮城県

MIYAGI

The third stop on our cross-country tour led us right through the city of Sendai, in the Miyagi Prefecture. We had gone to bed early the night before, so we were all well rested this time. Well, I mean, I'm always well rested, at least physically anyway, ha, ha, ha. Miyagi is known for having a lot of national parks, so we had our fair share of places to explore.

We decided to start by visiting the Osaki Hachimangu Shrine. Unfortunately, we were several days too early to experience the shrine's Establishment Day; but we still paid our respects regardless. I think it had been my favorite shrine thus far; it really was something to behold. The outside of the shrine was black as a raven, adorned with gold. The inside, while it couldn't be entered, carried the same theming. It really was incredible....

"While we're here, why don't we get some charms?" Kotarō asked, motioning to a spot where charms could be bought.

"Couldn't hurt," Makoto shrugged.

"Yeah!" Yuuki agreed.

They all made their way over to the stand and

perused the different options available; the sheer amount was staggering. Surprisingly enough, there were some pretty specific ones that were perfect for their current situation.

"What do you have there, Makoto?" Daichi asked, peering over at the robust boy as he studied a purple charm in his hand. "Oh," Makoto nonchalantly replied, holding up the charm. "It's just a traffic safety charm."

"Wow, wouldn't have expected there to be one for something like that," Daichi replied.

"How convenient," Minori added, leaning in to examine the small charm.

"Well, I figured it's a long trip, so it's not going to hurt to have it," Makoto chuckled.

"Here," Nakamura said from behind Daichi.

"Hm?" Daichi hummed, turning around to face the long-haired punk who held a charm between his fingers.

"What's this?" he asked, taking the small clear packet from Nakamura's fingers.

"You talk in your sleep," he replied.

"What?" Daichi shouted, mortified. He looked at Minori, who stood opposite him, behind Nakamura, almost as if he knew what was coming next. "Do I really?"

"Yeah," Nakamura replied, rubbing the back of his neck.

"I had no idea," Daichi cried. *God, this is so embarrassing!*

"To be fair, it's very seldomly, and usually, it's just complete nonsense," Minori shrugged.

"I haven't been able to make out what you've been rambling about, but the general idea seems to be about a loved one? Loving someone? I don't know. Something like that," Nakamura replied.

Daichi looked down at the charm he had taken from Nakamura. *This is for love?* he asked inwardly, studying

95

the characters on the little blue trinket.

"Anyway, maybe this'll help you out," Nakamura replied, sliding his hands into his pockets.

"Thanks, Nakamura," Daichi smiled, looking back up at the intimidating boy in front of him. "It's no big deal," Nakamura shrugged before walking away.

"I think Oda is starting to like you," Minori smiled.

"Hey, Daichi, did you find a charm?" Yuuki asked, joining him at his side.

"Sort of," he replied. "Nakamura found me one. What about you?"

"Sure did!" Yuuki beamed, showing off the charm he had picked and tied around his wrist.

"What's it for?" Daichi asked, examining the multicolored tassel.

"It's to ward off sickness," Yuuki eagerly replied.

"How very practical," Minori fondly smiled.

"Not a bad choice," Daichi commented.

"Yeah, well, I figured it couldn't hurt," Yuuki explained.

"Oh, yeah, you get sick a lot, huh, Yuuki?" Daichi asked, recalling that his classmate has missed a lot of days of school this year.

"Yeah," Yuuki shyly replied. "I have an auto-immune disorder, so unfortunately, it's just a part of my life."

"Sorry to hear that," Daichi earnestly replied.

"It's okay. It is what it is, you know?" Yuuki half-smiled.

"Yeah, I know all about having to come to terms with things you can't control," Daichi quietly admitted.

"All we can do is take it a day at a time," Yuuki replied. "That's what my dad says anyway."

"Hey, Yuuki, you find a charm, too?" Makoto asked, joining them, having concluded his business.

"Yup!" he replied, holding up his wrist again.

"Nice," Makoto complimented. "What about you, Daichi? You find anything?"

"Yeah," Daichi replied, holding up his charm.

"Which one did you get?" Yuuki asked, referring his question to Makoto.

"Just one for traffic safety," Makoto smiled.

"Good call!" Yuuki exclaimed.

"Yeah, I figured we've got a long way to go yet," Makoto replied. Daichi saw this as his moment to take his leave to pay for his charm, so he quietly slipped away as Makoto and Yuuki continued their conversation.

"Oh, searching for love?" the old lady running the stand asked as Daichi handed her his charm.

Daichi warily smiled, "I'm honestly not sure yet."

"That's when it happens," the old lady smiled, ringing up his trinket.

Daichi reached into his back pocket to retrieve his wallet when he felt a hand on his shoulder.

"I got it," Kotarō interjected. "Can we get these as well?" he asked, handing off a handful of charms to the old lady.

"Certainly," the snowy-haired woman replied gingerly, taking the small packaged trinkets from Kotarō. "Buying a few, I see," she politely noted.

"Yeah, I wanted to get some for my family," Kotarō replied.

"How very sweet of you," the nice lady smiled. "You know what they say, 'Do good for others and good will come to you'."

"Of course, that's how all of us should live," Kotarō replied, retrieving a colorful wallet from his back pocket.

"I could have paid for mine," Daichi noted, looking up at the relatively tall boy with long, jagged black hair.

97

"Kotarō does this all the time," Minori smiled as he crossed his arms.

"It's okay. You planned this whole trip, right?" Kotarō asked.

"I mean, that's one way of putting it, I guess," Daichi shrugged, not seeing his point. It wasn't like he really did much 'planning.'

"Well then, it's the least I can do," Kotarō smiled, taking a small plastic bag from the old lady running the stand. "We all wouldn't even be here if it weren't for you, Daichi." He reached into the bag and pulled Daichi's charm from it, handing it off to him. "Think of it as a thank you."

"Thanks, Kotarō," Daichi quietly replied. It was the first time he had called him by his first name since they had met, before they had left for the trip.

"Let's join the others," Kotarō suggested with an endearing smile.

"Oh, sure," Daichi agreed, his head snapping up to look at the soft-faced boy in front of him; if he hadn't known any better and under the right circumstances, Daichi wouldn't have been able to tell that Kotarō was a boy. He was really pretty.

"After you," Kotarō motioned with his free hand for Daichi to lead the way, returning his attention to the present.

"Everyone good to go?" Nakamura asked as the rest of the group joined him away from the charm stand.

"Ready," Yuuki beamed.

"Yeah, I'm good, unless there was something else anyone wanted to see," Makoto replied, checking with the rest of the group like a proper leader, which made sense, as he was the eldest. Daichi *may* have put the trip together, but Makoto was really the one making it happen. But the more he thought about it as he watched the others interact with one another, even watching Minori smile and laugh with them as they made jokes, he realized why they all got along so well. Each member of the band brought something to the table. They all complemented each other so well. Daichi had never really seen anything like it. His friends certainly weren't like this. It was like Nakamura had said weeks ago: they were a family. You could see it just by watching them.

Makoto was the eldest and the one primarily in charge of finding things for them to do.

Yuuki was the youngest and in the same class as Daichi, the only person he actually relatively knew; he was the one that kept everyone going.

Kotarō was like the mother of the group, making sure everyone was doing okay and was taken care of. He was in the same class as Minori had been, the class above Daichi.

Then there was Nakamura. Daichi wasn't exactly sure of anything when it came to him. He was, for all intents and purposes, the timekeeper of the trip, which came off as being done more out of habit than a conscious effort. He was also incredibly intimidating, if Daichi were being honest. He seemed loyal to his friends, but he also seemed like a loner and really reserved. It was kind of surprising that he was Minori's best friend. They seemed like polar opposites. He was also in the same class as Minori and Kotarō.

"Alright, let's get going, then," Nakamura said, reminding Daichi that there was a world outside the one in his own head.

The group agreed and made their way through the elegant row of giant red torii gates toward the entrance of the shrine, where they paid their respects one last time, as is customary, before leaving and continuing on their adventure.

After the shrine, we decided to go explore Dainohara Forest Park, which wasn't too far away, and it was massive! It was home to not just one but two different museums–a literature museum and a science museum.

The park even had a concert hall, which obviously, we were all very excited to see. It was absolutely stunning. The whole park was incredible. Even the literature museum–which we did not explore on the inside, as none of us were really readers–looked amazing from the outside.

The science museum had a circular section that loomed over a footpath, and if you were inside, you could look down onto the path from floor-to-ceiling windows. It was so awesome! I may have begged Daichi to go inside so that we could look out the windows, and like a true gentleman, he obliged. Of course, everyone had to come and see then, which prompted Yuuki to take various photos from both inside and outside. But that was as much of the museum as we experienced, ha, ha, ha. Scout's honor.

There was even a little shrine not too far from the literature museum, which–sidenote–sat behind a funeral home. We all thought that was equal parts bizarre and amusing for no reason other than its strangeness.

As was tradition, Daichi and I paid our respects at the itty-bitty shrine while the others made their way over to the lake on the opposite side of the park, behind the science museum.

"This park is so gigantic," Daichi breathed as he and Minori made their way to join the others.

"Biggest so far," Minori smiled.

"Man, I wish it weren't so hot. I may actually enjoy it," Daichi breathed.

"Hmm, you do appear a little sweaty," Minori noted.

"I don't suppose you can feel the heat, huh?" Daichi asked.

"'Fraid not," Minori shrugged.

"Then I guess I'll quit my complaining," Daichi smiled, placing his hands behind his head as a gentle breeze blew into him. "At least there's a breeze."

"Daichi," Minori said as he stopped moving.

"What's up?" Daichi asked, turning around to face his corporeal friend.

"Thank you," Minori smiled.

"It's no big deal. A little sweat never hurt anyone," Daichi replied, "at least I don't think so."

"That's not exactly what I meant," Minori chuckled.

"Oh? You're not thanking me for enduring this horrendous heat and humidity for your own amusement?" Daichi playfully asked.

"No, of course I am grateful for that as well," Minori laughed, a fond smile on his face. "I just meant, thank you for all of this." He motioned with his hand to the world around him. "Because of you, I'm having one last amazing adventure with my best friends."

"I didn't really do much," Daichi shrugged. "Nakamura is the real hero here."

"Maybe," Minori smiled. "But he's not my hero, Daichi."

Suddenly, Daichi's heart went into overdrive. He didn't deserve such praise! *What–Why do I feel this way? Do I?* Daichi let his hands fall to his side.

"You alright?" Minori asked.

Daichi snapped back to his senses. "Yeah, sorry, just…got distracted. Let's not keep the guys waiting," he replied with a nervous laugh, scratching the back of his head.

"Right, you know how Oda can get," Minori warmly smiled.

"Right," Daichi laughed, remembering their visit to the Fushimi Inari Shrine.

The two continued on their way through the park to meet with the others, coming across a rather elaborate playground for children.

"Whoa," Daichi chuckled as they passed through. "Would you get a load of this?"

"I've never been to a playground like this before," Minori commented; they came to a stop to get a better look at everything.

"Makes me wish I was still a kid," Daichi said.

"Yeah, me too," Minori chuckled.

"This is ridiculous," Daichi noted.

"Did you like going to playgrounds as a kid?" Minori asked as they watched a group of children run amok.

"More or less," Daichi laughed. "But that's probably pretty normal."

"Is it?" Minori asked, looking at Daichi.

"Well, sure. Didn't you go to the playground as a kid?" Daichi asked.

Minori stopped and thought it over. "Huh, not really," he replied.

"What'd you do for fun, then?" Daichi asked.

"To be honest...nothing," Minori replied.

"Huh?" Daichi peeped.

"I, uh—well, I grew up in a group home. I was adopted when I was nine, but up until then, it's not like I really did much, you know? Just met with families. Uh, I guess I don't really know," Minori explained shyly. That must sound silly. It's all kind of a blur, honestly."

"That's not silly," Daichi frowned.

"Maybe I can't remember because I'm dead," Minori mumbled, looking at his hands.

"Or," Daichi happily interjected, "you just don't want to remember."

"You think?" Minori asked, looking to Daichi.

"Sure," Daichi shrugged. "I'm sure it was a really hard time for you, so it'd make sense that you'd block out most of it."

"I guess that makes sense," Minori beamed, appearing relieved that he wasn't losing his memories. "Thanks, Daichi."

"I mean, it's my fault for even bringing it up," Daichi sheepishly smiled, ruffling the hair on the back of his head.

"Ah, it's okay," Minori lightheartedly replied, looking back at the kids playing. "I'm more or less over it now anyway. No point dwelling on it."

"Still," Daichi frowned.

"You can't miss what you never had, remember?" Minori asked.

Daichi smirked, nodding his head. "Right," he quietly agreed.

"Alright!" Minori exclaimed. "Let's keep going."

"Right, we have people waiting on us," Daichi nodded. "Can't afford to get too distracted."

"Cool playground, though," Minori commented, motioning with his hand.

"No doubt," Daichi agreed, before leading on.

Since it was a Monday, the science museum was actually closed, so after Daichi and I finally joined the others at the lake–

Well, I guess it was actually just a pond, though I suppose it could have just been a really tiny lake...

Anyway, we decided to start making our way back to the van, starting with a little honeycomb-shaped area just south of the museum, but not before Yuuki took some pictures of everyone around the ambiguous body of water

103

with a neat bridge running across it. Bridge is a loose term, though, as it was really just a path of stone slabs. Still, it was really cool, regardless of how you define it.

The honeycomb-shaped garden was really cool, too. You could actually see the industrial-looking science museum from it because they were side by side with one another. Looking at the museum, I don't know that you'd know that's what it was without being told; I certainly wouldn't have.

After we got back to the van, we decided to get something to eat at a sushi place next to the park. It was Makoto's pick. I've never been a big sushi fan–I can't stand the smell–but that wasn't really something I had to worry about anymore, ha, ha, ha.

There weren't a ton of hotel options around the park, so we decided to go about thirty minutes up the road to a cheap hotel near a public bath.

Let the record show that I am nothing if not a gentleman, so while the boys enjoyed the bath house, I enjoyed some R&R of my own in one of the many indoor relaxation chairs.

And just like that, our day in Miyagi more or less came to a close...

岩手県

IWATE

It was a three-hour drive from where we were in Sendai–Osawa, if you wanted to be a little more specific–to Tōno, where we would be spending the day.

We decided today's shrine would be the Unetori Shrine. It was a little thing tucked away between some trees. Red tags were used in abundance to signal its location in the pines. Despite its size, we treated it with the same reverence as all the others we'd visited thus far.

Nizato Atego Shrine was just a short walk away, so Daichi, Kotarō, and I decided to go pay our respects to it as well.

"You know you didn't have to come along, Kotarō," Daichi noted as they made their way to the other shrine, leaving the others to explore the area surrounding Unetori.

"Yeah, I know, but I wanted to come along," Kotarō smiled. "Gives us a chance to get to know one another better."

"That's fair," Daichi smiled.

"You know, they say Tōno is the birthplace of many of our folk tales," Kotarō stated as they made their way up a small set of stone stairs.

"Really?" Daichi asked.

"That's what they say," Kotarō smiled. "I actually read that they recount them at the museum not far from here."

"Wow," Daichi replied.

"I was going to ask the guys if they wanted to go check it out for ourselves," Kotarō explained.

"That could be cool," Daichi grinned, looking at the androgynous boy beside him.

"Cool, I'll ask the others when we get back," Kotarō smiled.

"Do you like old folk tales, Kotarō?" Daichi inquired.

"I'm more of a history buff," Kotarō sheepishly smiled. "But when you're the eldest of four, you get used to telling stories."

"Oh, really?" Daichi asked.

"I had no idea," Minori quietly admitted as he floated alongside them.

"I've actually never told anyone before," Kotarō fondly smiled. "Most of my siblings are older now, so I don't do it as much nowadays, but yeah, I used to have to tell a new story every night."

"Wow, talk about pressure," Daichi laughed.

"It's alright. Kept me learning new ones," Kotarō smiled.

"A new one every night, huh?" Daichi asked, looking up at the trees as he considered the implications.

"Yup," Kotarō chuckled.

"You ever think about writing stories of your own?" Daichi asked.

"Who would read them?" Kotarō chuckled.

"I mean, I would, and I don't even read much nowadays," Daichi replied, lacing his hands behind his head. "Don't get me wrong, I do my fair share of it, but I wouldn't call myself a *reader,* you know?"

107

"Sure, a casual partaker," Kotarō smiled.

"I mean, I've read less as I've gotten older," Daichi explained. "When I was younger, that was kind of all I did, that and video games."

"You didn't have many friends growing up, did you?" Kotarō politely asked.

"No, I guess not," Daichi chuckled. "I mean, I've always had friends. I just–I don't know–never really felt like I fit in with any of them."

"I can understand that," Kotarō replied. "I'm the same way. Well, I guess I was the same way until I met Minori and the others."

"Really?" Daichi smiled.

"Yeah, I mean up until that point, I spent a lot of time looking after my siblings. It wasn't until my second year of middle school, when I met Minori and Oda, that I really felt like I belonged somewhere," Kotarō elaborated. "And then we met Makoto that same year, and our little group grew by one. It feels like such a lifetime ago, even though it's only been a couple of years."

"Time sure flies, huh?" Daichi asked.

"I'll say," Kotarō smiled.

It didn't take the three terribly long to reach the foot of the shrine hidden within a sea of trees. The entrance was marked by two house-shaped posts that appeared to be lanterns, accompanied by some carved albino stones. A long, old stone staircase divided down the middle by a rope parted a small section of the green. From where they stood, they could see a red torii gate standing proudly, awaiting their arrival.

They made their way up the long set of stairs one stone brick at a time, stopping before the towering gate and paying their respects before entering the sacred grounds. Past the gate was another set of old stairs they took up to reach the shrine. Before paying their respects, they cleansed their hands with water provided by a small fountain just outside the shrine.

It wasn't the most avant-garde shrine they had visited, but it was nice. It was all one color for the most part–brown. Though the shrine's color was due to the lack of paint, thin pieces of trim were red, but they weren't very noticeable. What **was** noticeable, however, was the red railing that ran around the bottom of the shrine.

They didn't linger long. They silently paid their respects to the shrine nearly engulfed by trees, then began the walk back to their friends.

"How was it?" Makoto asked as Kotarō and Daichi returned to where they had initially left from.

"It was nice," Kotarō replied. "It wasn't anything crazy, but it was nice."

"Was it just a really small one or something?" Makoto inquired.

Kotarō and Daichi both looked at each other, making miscellaneous sounds as they determined the shrine's size.

"I mean, it wasn't *super* small or anything. I guess I'd say it was pretty standard," Daichi replied.

"Yeah, it was, I guess, a medium-sized shrine?" Kotarō added.

"You didn't miss out on anything, if that's what you're worried about," Daichi chuckled.

"Oh, okay, good. I kind of was starting to regret not going with you guys," Makoto sheepishly smiled.

"Yeah, it wasn't really anything to write home about," Kotarō smiled.

"Hey! How was it!?" Yuuki chimed as he and Nakamura joined the rest of them from some indiscernible location.

109

"They said it was okay," Makoto shrugged, looking over his shoulder at the small-statured, naturally brown-haired boy.

"Well, that's better than crappy!" Yuuki grinned.

"So, what's the plan now?" Nakamura asked.

"I was actually going to see if you guys would be interested in going to the Tōno Museum," Kotarō suggested. "Supposedly, it's dedicated to all the folklore stories of the city, and they even recount them live, from what I hear."

"That sounds cool!" Yuuki replied.

"It wouldn't hurt to check it out," Makoto shrugged.

"Whatever you guys want to do," Nakamura apathetically replied.

"Sounds like fun," Minori smiled.

"Yeah, I'm down," Daichi chimed.

The Museum: Tōno Story of The Mansion, as it was called, was surprisingly great. Daichi had been a little skeptical, if he were being honest, but the whole thing turned out to be really fun.

The museum itself was in the heart of the city, so after they had finished at the museum, they had their pick of things to do. There was even another museum not that far away, dedicated specifically to the city. Since Kotarō was the resident historian, he talked them all into checking it out, which no one really seemed to mind. It wasn't like the rest of them had any other ideas—not even Makoto, who normally was in charge of activities.

The Tōno City Museum was what you'd expect: a couple old kabuki masks, some very old paintings, tools and weapons. Nothing particularly remarkable, at least not to Daichi. Kotarō was having a blast, though, and that was all that really mattered. There was a neat village diorama that he and Minori spent a fair time examining. It wasn't nearly as big as the one at the railway museum back home, but it was still neat nonetheless.

After the second museum of the day, Yuuki picked a place for them to go and eat; he picked a small ramen shop up the road, where the five of them practically filled it to capacity. It was a homey place with small bookshelves packed with plenty of tankōbon to read. After they finished eating, they took a moment to sit and read for a bit since they were already there and weren't being shooed off. They were sure to order more drinks as they read, though, so they weren't just taking space at the bar.

"So, what now?" Nakamura asked as they exited the tiny ramen shop.

"Well, let's see what we've got around here," Makoto said, pulling out his phone from his front pocket and sliding his thumb across the glass screen, bringing it to life. It took him a moment to pull up a map on his phone, but he quickly got to work scouring the surrounding area for things to do. "Dude, I have never seen so many spots to eat in one place before," he commented aloud as he moved his thumb around the screen of his phone.

"Really?" Yuuki asked, moving in close to him to get a look for himself. "Wow, that *is* a lot of places!"

"Well, there's the Nabekura Castle Ruins," Makoto said as he studied his phone.

"That could be fun," Daichi shrugged.

"I'm cool with whatever," Nakamura replied as he slid his hands into the pockets of his black skinny jeans.

"Alright," Makoto said. "It's only a fifteen-minute walk from here. Oh, and Daichi, there's two shrines near it, too."

"Awesome!" Daichi exclaimed.

"Man, you really love shrines, huh?" Nakamura asked.

111

"Hey, I'll take all the blessings I can get," Daichi chuckled.

"Hey, I'll go with you, if you want!" Yuuki chimed.

"Sure, if you want to," Daichi grinned.

"Alright then, let's get going," Makoto said as he slid his phone back into his pocket. "The castle is just past the city museum."

Daichi and I ended up actually going to three shrines before reaching the castle: Nanbu Shrine, Ichijo Inari Shrine, and Taga Shrine.

Since Chionji Temple was on the way to the castle observatory as well, we all decided to visit it together. There wasn't too much to see, but it was still a fun experience. Since both Ichijo Shrine and Nanbu Shrine were on the way as well, we all visited those two together.

Nanbu Shrine sat atop a hill overlooking Tōno. It was nice. It had plenty of space at the base of the shrine; Kotarō said the space was used for demonstrations.

Ichijo Inari Shrine was a little shrine that sat right beside the Nanbu Shrine. It was kind of funny seeing this humble shrine next to the behemoth that was Nanbu Shrine.

After we all took a look at the temple, Daichi and I parted from the group to visit Taga Shrine. The Taga Shrine was interesting; it, too, shared its holy ground with other smaller shrines. However, these shrines were itty-bitty, like the kind we sometimes saw alongside a road or maybe in a park. There weren't two but three of them!

The Taga Shrine itself didn't look anything like the shrines we had visited up till that point. It looked kind of modern. Sure, it was visibly a shrine, but gone were the extravagant tiered clay shingle roof and ornate wood carvings adorning it. It just had a simple wooden sign, with a red-and-white striped banner below. It was elevated from the ground by these almost cylindrical stones, making it appear as though it had been moved there from somewhere else. The stairs leading up to the sliding glass doors of the shrine were half stone and half wood, both looking weathered and worn. On the right side of the shrine, there was a nice set of dark wooden stairs that led to a very modern-looking sliding door. The top half of the door was glass, while the lower half was screen. It almost appeared like an addition had been built onto the shrine.

"What a peculiar shrine," Minori noted with his hand to his chin as he and Daichi stood in front of the shrine; it almost looked like a tiny house.

"Yeah, I was just thinking the same thing," Daichi replied.

"It's quaint, though," Minori smiled.

"It's definitely unique," Daichi chuckled. "Makoto is going to be mad he missed it."

"It's too bad Yuuki isn't here to take a picture," Minori joked with a look of fondness.

"I've got him covered," Daichi replied, retrieving his phone from his front pocket.

"How sweet of you," Minori smiled.

Daichi's heart was sent into a fury for a moment by the beautiful ghost's words.

"Naw, he'd do the same for me," Daichi smiled, taking a picture of the shrine.

"That doesn't change anything, by my estimations," Minori replied.

"Ha, ha, ha, I don't think that word means what you think it means swee–Minori," Daichi replied, his heart in a panic. *I almost called him sweetie! What is wrong with me?* he internally screamed. He casually glanced Minori's way to see if he had noticed. He stood with his arms crossed, looking over the shrine in front of them. *Okay, calm down. It looks like he didn't notice,* Daichi thankfully noted.

After Daichi took a few pictures for Yuuki and the guys, we paid our respects to the three tiny shrines nearby and left to meet up with the others.

The castle observatory was nice. It was surprisingly short and sat secluded atop a hill, hidden away amongst a sea of trees, its only companion a tall white pillar that featured a winged creature proudly standing at the tip. But the best part was that we had it all to ourselves.
From the top of the pagoda-style tower, you could see what looked like all of Tōno. Though our time at the top of the world was short, it was absolutely incredible....

青森県

AOMORI

"That should do it," Nakamura said as he finished staking Daichi's tent to the soft earth beneath their feet.

"I didn't know you knew how to camp," Daichi said as Nakamura stood up from the ground.

"Yeah, I was in Cub Scouts as a kid," the punk rock-looking boy replied.

"That's actually how Oda and I met," Minori smiled. "My parents thought it would help me to make some friends, which *apparently*, it did, even if the only friend I made was him."

"That's actually how Minori and I met," Nakamura said as he massaged the back of his neck.

"I would have never guessed," Daichi chuckled.

"Yeah. Minori hated camping," Nakamura breathed, sliding his hands into his front pockets.

"Yeah, that sounds like him," Daichi smiled.

"Bugs are gross," Minori muttered, crossing his arms.

"So I told him not to worry, because I would look out for him," Nakamura warily smiled. "He was like a second brother to me."

"Was Rory in Scouts with you guys?" Daichi asked,

thinking it over.

"Yeah, so really, I was looking after two people instead of just one," Nakamura sighed, sounding exhausted.

"Sounds like a handful," Daichi grinned.

"Minori certainly was, but you know what, as we got older, Rory got pretty independent," Nakamura smiled. "He certainly doesn't need me anymore."

"I wouldn't say that," Daichi frowned.

"It's okay. I'm glad," Nakamura fondly smiled. "There's no better feeling as an older brother than knowing that you've helped prepare your younger sibling for the world ahead."

"I didn't realize Rory was younger than you," Daichi replied.

"Only by a year," Nakamura shrugged. "But still, that does make me the older sibling, and if you had known Rory before, you would understand."

"Rory used to be pretty timid," Minori smiled.

"Yeah, that makes sense," Daichi agreed.

"Anyway, I better go set up the other tents, seeing as I'm the *only one* who knows how to do it," Nakamura said, looking away toward the others, who were all very clearly struggling to set up the other tents.

"Do you need any help?" Daichi asked.

"Did you suddenly learn how to do it?" Nakamura asked, raising a brow.

"Well, no," Daichi sheepishly replied.

"Then no," Nakamura said as he took his leave. "I can handle it fine myself," he waved as the distance between them grew.

It had been his suggestion that they all go camping while in Aomori since they had all the necessary gear with them and it would have been a waste to go the whole trip without using it. Daichi had never gone camping before, so

117

he had no reason to say no. And after Nakamura outed him to the others as someone who talks in their sleep, they all agreed to let him have his own tent, which meant Daichi could finally spend the night talking with Minori as he usually did before the trip.

Nakamura had said he didn't think of it at the time but that Miyagi would have been the best place to have gone camping; being it was known for having so many national parks. The timing didn't seem right, though, so they all agreed to go camping today to make up for it. After all, it was the only thing they could think of that Nakamura had suggested they do the whole trip thus far.

They had decided to make camp at Utarube Camping Ground, as it seemed like the perfect location. It was right next to Lake Towada and not far from Kojimaga Ura; plus, Towada Shrine was just up the road from them.

"Now that we're all set up, you want to go pay our respects at the shrine?" Daichi asked, referring his question to Minori.

"It's quite a walk. Are you sure *you* want to?" Minori smiled.

"It beats standing around here," Daichi shrugged. "Nakamura is gonna be busy setting up the other tents for a while," he joked.

"Yeah, it's a shame I'm not alive. I could be helping him," Minori replied, his arms gently crossed in front of him.

"Do you even remember how to do it?" Daichi chuckled.

"More or less," Minori smiled. "I'd certainly fare better than the others."

"Yeah, I guess that's true," Daichi admitted as he watched Nakamura chastise the others. "I guess I better let them know we're leaving for a bit."

"Yeah, wouldn't want them to worry," Minori agreed.

"Hey, I'm going to go take a walk up to the shrine!"

Daichi called, his hands forming a funnel in front of his mouth to amplify his voice.

"Okay!" Yuuki shouted, waving back.

"Be careful!" Kotarō added before going back to helping Nakamura with the tent setup.

The walk to the shrine was twenty minutes, which wasn't great, but Daichi figured it'd probably take the group an hour to get the other tents set up anyway. It wasn't too hot today, so he figured he should take advantage of it. And it was more alone time with Minori, which he was grateful for. They passed a whopping four inns, as well as one public bathroom, along their walk before reaching the tucked-away shrine.

If Minori hadn't noticed the weathered white torii gate when they had driven by earlier, they likely would have never found it. There were no pictures of it on the internet, and the name it bore was the same as another shrine south of where they were camping, making it impossible to pull up any sort of information about. It was almost as though the shrine itself was in hiding, concealed away under the cover of the woods behind a couple of old sheds beside the road.

Regardless, Daichi enjoyed their little excursion together. They didn't dilly-dally, but they did talk a lot. It was almost like they couldn't talk fast enough, or maybe it was just Daichi who was talking quickly. He didn't get many opportunities during the trip to just talk with Minori like he did before, so he wanted to make sure he took advantage of every moment of their time alone together.

Daichi actually found himself a little bummed as the two of them returned to the campsite where the others were waiting for him. He wished he could have just had a little bit more time alone with Minori. It actually made him wish the end of the day would come fast so they could just

119

lie around and talk with one another some more. It was such an odd feeling, but he decided he was going to question how he felt less and embrace it more; he hoped it would be less confusing that way.

The rest of the day continued how one would expect a day of camping to go. They explored more of the forest around them, specifically Mikurahan Island, which was a peninsula in the middle of Lake Towada. They made sure to make time to visit Kankodai, which had an amazing view of the lake. They saved it for last so they could view it at sunset, giving them just enough time to make it back to the campsite before it got too dark.

Of course, once again, the group relied on Nakamura's Cub Scouts talents to start the campfire, though they did help with collecting firewood.

"If you had told me a few weeks ago, we'd all be up camping together in Towada, I would have told you, you were crazy," Kotarō fondly smiled as he watched the fire crackle.

"I was just thinking the same thing," Makoto smiled.

"I'm really happy we are," Yuuki quietly replied.

"It's too bad we're one man short," Kotarō frowned.

"But we have the next best thing," Yuuki smiled looking at Daichi.

"Yeah, man, we owe you," Makoto smiled as he, too, shifted his attention to Daichi.

"You guys don't owe me anything," he softly replied. "I'm the one who owes you guys. I can't tell you how grateful I am that you guys agreed to come along."

"Yeah, well, it's not like we could have let you just go alone with Oda," Makoto teased as he leaned back, bracing himself with his hands.

"*Ha ha*," Nakamura dryly replied, poking the fire with a long stick.

"I think—I think Minori is here with us in spirit,"

Daichi quietly replied as he watched the fire flicker and dance before his eyes, his arms wrapped around his legs, his knees under his chin. "I can't explain it, but I know he is."

"Daichi, I–," Minori began to speak.

"I feel the same way," Kotarō softly interjected.

"Yeah, I can't really explain it, but me too!" Yuuki eagerly agreed.

"You guys," Minori breathed.

"I sure hope he is, for all the work I'm doing," Nakamura muttered.

"You? What about me?" Makoto replied. "I'm the one doing all the driving!"

The group, with the exception of Nakamura, burst into laughter; even Minori joined in.

"Even if he isn't," Kotarō said as he looked up at the starry sky above, "I hope wherever he is, he can see us."

"I'm sure he can," Daichi gently smiled in response, glancing the spirit's way.

"Thanks, Daichi," Kotarō smiled back.

"He'd probably think we were crazy," Nakamura half-smiled, but it was still a smile. "I wonder what he would say."

"I almost wouldn't be surprised if he were mad that we went without him," Makoto laughed.

"Don't say that!" Yuuki whined.

"If Daichi hadn't told me it was his final wish, I'd probably believe that," Nakamura replied, still smiling.

"Yeah," Makoto replied. "I'm sure wherever Minori is, he's doing just fine."

"Most days," Minori fondly smiled.

"Well, I'm gonna head to bed," Nakamura groaned, standing up from his spot on the ground.

"Really?" Yuuki asked.

"Yeah, we've got a big day tomorrow, and I want to

121

make sure I get *some* sleep tonight," Nakamura replied, throwing his stick into the fire. "Be sure to let that die down before you guys go to bed," he added, motioning to the fire with his hand.

"Yeah, we will," Makoto assured.

"Good. I don't need you guys somehow setting the forest on fire," Nakamura replied before leaving for the tent he was sharing with Kotarō.

"I guess I'll head to bed, too, then," Daichi said, slowly getting up from his spot.

"You too, huh?" Makoto asked.

"Yeah, I've never slept outside before, so figure it's better to try and get to sleep sooner than later," Daichi reasoned, which was true for the most part. On the one hand, he was eager to have Minori to himself; on the other, he really did want to make sure he wasn't up too late.

"I'll join you in a bit," Minori smiled up at him from the ground.

Daichi was a little caught off guard and, honestly, maybe even a little bummed, but he understood.

The other two wished Daichi a good night, and he headed over to his tent a couple of feet away. As he left, he heard both Makoto and Yuuki mention that neither of them were the least bit tired, so it was good that Nakamura had the foresight to bunk them together.

Daichi didn't have his tent to himself for long. Minori came phasing inside, startling him.

"You scared me," Daichi chuckled. "Are the others going to bed now, too?"

"Naw, I just got bored," Minori smiled, lying down on the sleeping bag Daichi had rolled out for him. "Turns out, hanging out around a campfire is actually pretty lackluster when nobody can hear you," he chuckled as he studied the thin ceiling.

"That makes sense," Daichi groaned as he slid into his sleeping bag.

"Don't get me wrong, it was nice for a little bit, but...well, I had my fill," Minori said, finishing with a laugh. "So I figured, hey, why not spend time with someone who can actually hear me?"

"I'm flattered," Daichi chuckled.

"Well, don't be too flattered; the choices were me or you," Minori grinned.

"Fair enough," Daichi laughed. "Hey, a win is a win."

"My dad used to say if you're not cheating, then you're not playing to win," Minori replied. "It doesn't quite apply to this situation, but you reminded me of that."

"Hey, Minori, I have been meaning to ask you something," Daichi said, briefly adjusting his position.

"Shoot," Minori smiled, only briefly glancing Daichi's way.

"Do ghosts sleep?" Daichi asked, looking up at the ceiling of the tent. "Or do you just spend the night watching me sleep?"

"I think watching someone sleep is frowned upon unless you're married," Minori replied with a laugh.

"I don't think it's weird if you're a couple," Daichi proposed, looking over at the pale figure lying on the ground beside him.

"Oh, we're a couple now?" Minori playfully asked.

"I–Well–I mean–," Daichi tripped over his words as his face grew hot. *I didn't mean that! I mean, like, I guess I've thought about it, but that's weird! I mean weird for me! I'm not gay! Sure, I mean, I've never dated anyone before, but I'd know if I liked Minori that way, wouldn't I?* Daichi internally argued with himself.

"I'm just kidding, Daichi," Minori chuckled. "No need to get all upset."

123

"I'm not upset!" Daichi instinctively protested.

"Oh, my...Daichi robbing the grave, how bold of you," Minori slyly taunted.

"I didn't mean it like that!" Daichi retorted.

"Could have fooled me," Minori smugly smiled, looking up at the flimsy yellow ceiling above them.

"I just–You know what I meant!" Daichi shouted.

"Of course I did," Minori chuckled. "I'm only messing with you, Daichi. Besides, even if you felt that way, it's not like it would matter."

"W-What do you mean?" Daichi quietly asked, his heart aflutter. *Does Minori not feel how I feel? I mean, does he not like-like me like that? I mean, that's fine! It's not like, you know, I'm wanting to date him...I mean...I like Minori, but as a friend! I just really admire him is all. That's completely normal!* Daichi's internal monologue spiraled out of control in the time it took for Minori to reply.

"There's no future with me," Minori answered before glancing over to Daichi with a smile.

"Oh," Daichi frowned. "Yeah, I guess that makes sense."

"After our trip is finished, I'm sure I'll leap, or whatever it's called," Minori smiled as he looked back up at the ceiling.

"I don't think it's called that," Daichi laughed as he studied the features of Minori's face.

"Oh, what would you call it, then?" Minori asked, glancing from the corners of his eyes at Daichi.

"I don't know, but not leaping," Daichi smiled. "And you never answered my question."

"What was the question again?" Minori asked, looking back at the mousy-haired boy.

"Do you dream? Or, like, sleep? Or have you just been spending the nights together watching me sleep?" Daichi asked.

"Yes, yes, and, if you promise not to be mad, sometimes," Minori replied, laughing at the last bit.

"I knew it!" Daichi exclaimed.

"I'm kidding!" Minori burst into laughter. "I would never do that to someone I wasn't dating."

"But if we were," Daichi expounded, his heart suddenly quickening its pace again. *My heart is racing again…*he silently noted.

"Sure, *if* we were, then I would absolutely watch you while you slept, maybe. At least once. Again, I think that's more of a marriage thing," Minori smiled, playing along with Daichi's hypothetical.

"Okay, fine, if we were married, then!" Daichi retorted, his heart still violently pumping away, each contraction and expansion reverberating inside his skull reminding him of his volatile feelings.

"I hate to break it to you, Daichi, but we'd never be married," Minori coyly replied.

"Yeah, okay, I know the no-future thing, whatever. I mean hypothetically," Daichi prattled through, trying to just get an answer.

"That's not it," Minori chuckled before fixing his gaze on the almost ordinary-looking boy beside him. "It's illegal for gays to–or, I guess in our case, two men to be married in Japan," he casually elaborated.

"Wait, really?" Daichi asked in shock. *I figured maybe a long time ago, gay people wouldn't have been able to get married, but I had assumed that was just a long time ago,* Daichi thought to himself.

"Yeah, so even *if* I were still alive and even *if* you had agreed to go out with me, we still wouldn't have been able to get married. It's a shame, really," Minori replied.

"Why do you say that?" Daichi forced out of his mouth. Each *if* of Minori's sentence had kicked him straight in the heart; the word felt burned into his brain.

125

"Because our wedding would have been spectacular," Minori smiled, looking up at the less-than-spectacular view. "You know, hypothetically," he casually added with a shrug of his shoulders.

Daichi propped himself up with his elbow. "Okay then, so what *if*," he began to suggest, his heart setting into overdrive now—it felt as though it would burst forth from his chest at this rate—"we got married, hypothetically, somewhere else?"

"Like where?" Minori chuckled, appearing amused by the game they were playing.

"I don't know. Let's say America; it's legal there, right?" Daichi asked, motioning with his free hand to Minori.

"I'm not sure," Minori replied, thinking it over. "Sounds like it would be."

"Great, okay, for the sake of the argument, let's say it is," Daichi quickly stated again, just trying to get a clear answer from Minori so his heart could stop racing.

"Oh, we're arguing? How authentic," Minori slyly responded as he, too, rolled onto his side and propped himself up with his elbow, placing himself at Daichi's eye level.

"Just—Gah! Go with it, okay?" Daichi asked, audibly flustered.

"I'm with you, darling. Continue," Minori politely replied, sounding as if he were doing his best stay-at-home-wife impression. Even if he were joking, the way he said *darling* made Daichi's stomach sink lower than he thought possible. "I'm just trying to get into character," Minori playfully added, his free hand acting as a sort of flipper.

"Fine," Daichi replied, rolling his eyes. *Almost there,* he told himself. He felt as though the end was in sight. "Right, so if we got married somewhere else."

"America," Minori interjected.

"Right, America," Daichi waved off.

"But where?" Minori asked, squinting his eyes.

"W-What does it matter?" Daichi stammered, clearly not as into the game as Minori.

"If we're going down the hypothetical road, I want to be able to play it out as much as possible," Minori replied, his inner diva that Nakamura had talked about finally showing its face.

"Fine," Daichi shortly replied. "You pick."

"Hmmm, California," Minori quickly replied.

"Okay, sure," Daichi just as quickly shot back.

"Great," Minori nodded. And just as Daichi went to speak again, Minori cut him off. "What season were you thinking? Because I was thinking spring. Ooo, unless we want a winter wedding!" He let out a loving sigh before quickly continuing, "I love the snow. Never mind. Changed my mind. I want a winter wedding, so California is out. Pretty sure it doesn't snow there. Somewhere else in America, with snow."

Daichi let out an exasperated sigh. At least Minori's rambling had allowed his heart to settle down.

"Okay, fine," he replied as politely as he could muster.

"Great," Minori smiled. "I'm thinking an open bar. What about you?"

"We can't even drink!" Daichi replied.

"Well, yeah, we can't right now, but we're talking about the hypothetical future, right?" Minori asked.

Daichi let out a heavy sigh. "Yeah, alright, sure," he agreed.

"Sure to which? Open bar or the future?" Minori asked. "Or both?"

"Both," Daichi muttered.

"Great!" Minori beamed.

"Anything else?" Daichi asked.

"How would our family get there? Or would we even invite our families?" Minori asked. "Not sure about yours, but I'm sure after the initial shock and adjustment period, my family would accept my being gay."

"Yeah, I'm not so sure about mine," Daichi sheepishly replied. "They're pretty old-fashioned."

"Yeah, I did get that vibe from them," Minori agreed as he appeared to think it over in his head. "Okay, so my family; likely not yours. What about our friends?" he inquired.

"Uh, yeah, sure. I think Hayashi and Matsuda would still accept me," Daichi replied briefly, thinking it over in his head.

"Great, and obviously, the band would support it, so there's them, too," Minori smiled, very clearly planning out the imaginary wedding in his head.

"Great, so if we did get married," Daichi proposed slowly, waiting for another outburst from Minori, which, to his surprise, didn't come.

"Uh-huh," Minori politely nodded.

"Would you then be comfortable watching me sleep?" Daichi asked.

"Well, it really doesn't matter what I'm comfortable with," Minori nonchalantly replied, warranting a verbal reaction from Daichi.

"Huh?" Daichi almost squawked, his voice becoming nasally.

"Well, I mean, you're the one being watched, right? Not much say I would really have in the matter," Minori chuckled.

"The whole point was that you wouldn't be comfortable with it unless we were married!" Daichi shouted.

"No, no," Minori wiggled his finger. "I said *most*

people. You happened to assume I was one of those people.”

“Ugh! What does that mean!” Daichi retorted, leaning closer to Minori, using his hands to brace himself.

“Meaning,” Minori replied, “I’d watch you even if we were only dating if it were okay with you,” he slyly added as he closed the gap between them, his corporeal face only inches from Daichi’s. If he were alive, he would have felt Daichi’s breath.

Daichi’s heart burst back to life with renewed vigor; the only logical move was for Daichi to just let himself drop to the floor, so he did, landing with a soft but audible thump. He’d gladly accept the pain over the possibility of Minori hearing his heart run amok.

“Oh, my,” Minori replied. “Are you alright, Daichi?”

“I’m good,” Daichi replied, the earth beneath their tent muffling his voice. His ears were on fire! The pain he felt from hitting the floor was a small price to pay to hide his burning face.

“What are you doing?” Minori inquired.

“I’m–” Daichi began to reply when he suddenly remembered he had literally no excuse prepared.

“You’re…?” Minori slowly coaxed.

“Exhausted,” Daichi uttered in defeat.

“Huh, I see,” Minori softly replied.

“What do you dream about?” Daichi asked, his face still barricaded from Minori by his arms.

“Just what my life would have been like if I hadn’t died,” Minori softly answered, his voice like velvet.

That must suck, Daichi quietly noted. *Sounds like every night must be a nightmare for him, but if I’m being honest, I’ve had a lot of dreams recently about the same thing.* “I’m sorry.” Daichi frowned as he sat up. “That–That must be really tough. I had no idea.”

“It’s okay,” Minori fondly smiled. “It’s kind of nice. I

mean, I get to viscerally feel what could have been instead of just thinking or talking about it."

"I guess," Daichi quietly agreed.

"Sure, it's a little bit of a bummer when I wake up to realize it was all just a dream, but...I think I would rather have the dreams than not have them. I suppose that's kind of silly now that I say it out loud," Minori explained, finishing with a sheepish laugh.

"I don't think so," Daichi whispered.

Minori chuckled, "It's alright. You can tell me it's silly."

Daichi shook his head in opposition. "But it's not," he replied. "It's only natural. I mean, I think it would be kind of weird if you *didn't* dream about if you were still alive. I think if the dreams bring you any sort of comfort or joy, it's good that you have them."

"I'll keep that in mind," Minori smiled as he rolled onto his back and looked up at the illuminated ceiling.

"Well," Daichi groaned as he stretched out his arms. "I guess we should probably get some sleep."

"Yeah, big day tomorrow," Minori smiled. "Hokkaido, last stop of the trip."

"Well, last stop of the first round," Daichi smiled as he reached up to the hanging lantern of their tent to turn it off. "We still have the trip back to look forward to."

Daichi switched off the lantern and laid back down on his side to face Minori, who laid atop an unrolled baby-blue sleeping bag. "Wait!" Minori suddenly shouted causing Daichi to jump. "What?!" he frantically replied his heart having nearly come up out his bottom. "For our wedding what do you think about me wearing a dress?" Minori thoughtfully asked.

Daichi rolled his eyes letting out a sigh, "seriously?"

Minori let out a little amused laugh, "sorry, sorry, I'll stop.".

"You're unbelievable," Daichi chuckled rolling over onto his side.

"Good night, Daichi," Minori softly replied, his voice warm, like how Daichi imagined a lover to sound. His heart would have skipped a beat if it wasn't already beating out of his chest from Minori's little stunt. "Good night Minori," he breathed in response settling his hair-trigger heart. And with that final exchange the young teen eased into a blissful slumber as the cicadas sang into the night around them.

I know it was just hypothetically, but.... imagining a life where Daichi and I got married....

It made me immeasurably happy.

北海道

HOKKAIDO

"We're almost there," Daichi noted as he and Minori stood beside the railing of the ferry that glided upon the water, bound for their more or less final stop, Hokkaido.

"Crazy, right?" Minori chuckled. "But you did it. You pulled it off."

"Well, I wouldn't say that yet; we'll still need to get back," Daichi replied.

"If there's a back," Minori quietly replied. "I don't think there will be, not for me."

Daichi glanced away, studying the waves as they crashed against the ship; his heart ached. He didn't want to think about him and Minori parting ways. He knew they would have to and that the whole point of the trip was for it to be one final huzzah–the last push to get him to the other side–but…he didn't want him to go. They had missed out on so much time together. It wasn't fair. If he had known life could have been like this, *he* would have been the one to go out of his way to talk to Minori, invite him to hang out, go see his band play.

"Let's make this our best day together yet," Minori smiled, his soft voice refocusing Daichi's attention to his face.

"Absolutely!" Daichi chimed.

"We're almost there, dude," Makoto said, coming up from behind Daichi.

"Yeah," Daichi smiled, glancing back at the boy who looked like he could be an American hockey player.

"Crazy to think," Makoto replied. "Hokkaido seemed so far away at the start, and now we are literal hours away."

"Yeah," Daichi laughed. "I've got to admit, I wasn't sure how this would work out."

"Hmmm, and yet you were always so confident about it," Minori fondly smiled, casting his gaze at Daichi.

"Well–" Daichi began to reply, quickly catching himself. "All I knew was I had to make it happen, for Minori."

"Well, you did it, man," Makoto smiled with his hands in the pockets of his white basketball shorts.

The three sat in silence for a bit, just watching the horizon. Minori decided he wanted to go see what the others were up to, as it had been a while since they had last seen them. And while Daichi's heart, for a lack of a better word, beckoned him to follow almost instinctively, he did have something he had been toying around with asking Makoto, or anyone at this point, really. He could have asked his mom during one of his regular check-ins, but he thought it'd be more than a little awkward.

After Minori had moved out of earshot, Daichi looked to the stalwart boy who was silently enjoying the view beside him.

"Hey, Makoto, can I ask you something?" Daichi politely inquired.

"Hm? Sure, what is it?" Makoto asked, looking over at Daichi, seemingly a little caught off guard.

"This is going to sound a little weird, but I'm not really sure who else to ask at this point, and I kind of need

135

to know as soon as possible, but, uh, how do you know if you like someone?" Daichi asked.

"Oh, man!" Makoto exclaimed, his body twisting and turning. "Uh, let's see...How do I know if I like someone?" he asked for clarification.

"Sure," Daichi shrugged.

"I don't know. I guess I've never really even thought about it before. Give me a sec," Makoto replied, visibly mulling over the question in his mind.

"I'm sorry. I didn't mean to put you on the spot," Daichi laughed.

"I guess you just know," Makoto replied. "Like for me, it isn't very complicated. Like, either I like the person and want to be with them or I just don't have those feelings, you know?"

"Hmm, I see," Daichi quietly replied, thinking it over himself.

"I don't know. I hope that helps, dude," Makoto shrugged. "If Minori were here, I'd tell you to ask him. He was always surrounded by girls, so the guy must have been doing something right," he finished with a laugh.

"Yeah, he certainly was popular with the girls," Daichi smiled.

"Well, I'm going to go look for the others, make sure they haven't gotten into too much trouble," Makoto said, beginning to take his leave.

"Oh! Okay, I'll come, too," Daichi replied, following behind.

It didn't take the two boys long to find the others on the rather large ferryboat. They had been sitting down inside. It turned out Kotarō had gotten seasick; it was surprising to not just the others but Kotarō himself as well. While Yuuki and Nakamura sat on one of many blue benches, Kotarō laid on his back beside them.

"So, what's the plan for when we reach Hokkaido?" Nakamura asked. "I mean, I'm all for winging it like the other places, but I feel like if this is supposed to be the whole point of the trip, we need to make it count."

"Well, Hokkaido is known for its milk," Kotarō groaned from the floor.

"Okay, what else?" Nakamura asked, not bothering to look down at the shambles of a boy on the floor.

"Well, there's supposed to be this, like, White Lovers chocolate that you can only find there, and it's supposed to be really good," Kotarō elaborated further.

"White Lovers chocolate?" Daichi asked, his ears perking up. He leaned over to peer down at his sickly friend on the floor.

"Yeah, it's supposed to be really good. Actually, I've heard all the food in Hokkaido is a cut above the rest," Kotarō explained.

"Okay, so we're definitely eating as much food as we can," Nakamura said, taking charge of the trip planning. "What else, Kotarō?"

"Uh, well, there's Daisetsuzan National Park," Kotarō sighed, placing an arm over his face.

"That could be cool," Makoto suggested.

"Yeah, wouldn't hurt to check out. Okay, so food, park, anything else?" Nakamura asked, finally glancing down behind him to his friend.

"Sapporo is the capital, so we probably should check that out, too; it'd probably be the best place to check out all the different snacks and maybe any exclusive foods we can't get back home," Kotarō warily explained.

"Yeah, that'd make sense," Makoto said, looking at Nakamura.

"There's also Mt. Yōtei, which people say bears a resemblance to Mt. Fuji," Kotarō gulped.

"Okay, so mountain, *Sapporo*, then park?" Makoto

asked, relaying his question to Nakamura, as they were clearly the ones in charge of coordinating the trip.

"Yeah, that sounds good to me. We can always add on more once we get there, too," Nakamura replied.

"That sounds good to me," Yuuki chimed.

"Yeah, sounds fun," Daichi agreed.

"I concur. Sounds like a lovely time," Minori smiled. "I would say I'm surprised, but Oda and Makoto *were* always the ones to make sure we got to the gigs on time, and Oda always took charge helping to set up our gear and equipment when it was our turn to play."

"I can't wait! This is going to be so awesome!" Yuuki exclaimed.

"Yeah, I can't wait to be off this boat either," Kotarō muttered, sending the group into a small fit of laughter.

Kotarō didn't have to suffer much longer before we were back on dry land and heading to our first stop in Hokkaido. We didn't stop to explore Mt. Yōtei, but we did admire it from afar as we drove. We all wondered what the view must have been like from the top as it loomed over us in the distance.

It was over a four-hour drive from where the ferry had dropped us off in Hokkaido to Sapporo, though part of that was us stopping for lunch at a zanki restaurant. The legends were true: everything tastes better in Hokkaido! To be fair, zanki is a specialty of Hokkaido, but if you ask me, it still counts.

After a grueling car ride, we finally made it—the promised land, Sapporo, the land of excellent food, capital of Hokkaido. And it was stunning…

"Hey, so I don't mean to alarm anyone, but...we've made it to Sapporo!" Nakamura eagerly proclaimed. The rest of the group cheered in excitement.

"Finally," Daichi breathed a sigh of relief.

"I almost thought we'd never make it," Yuuki whined.

"So, what's first?" Kotarō asked.

"Dude, we've got us covered," Makoto said, motioning between him and Nakamura.

"You guys figured out what we're gonna do?" Daichi asked, a little surprised they had planned what to do already.

"Well, yeah, we weren't just going to sit in the car for four hours with nothing to show for it," Makoto laughed.

"Yeah, somebody needed to take charge," Nakamura added.

"We think we should visit Hokkaido Jingu Shrine first. If everyone is up for it afterwards, there's a zoo within walking distance we could check out," Makoto suggested.

"Okay, that sounds good to me," Daichi agreed.

"Man, I haven't been to a zoo in so long!" Yuuki exclaimed.

"Yeah, it's been a minute since I've gone to one as well," Kotarō replied.

"Come to think of it, I can't remember the last time I went," Minori added, sitting beside Yuuki in the back row of the vehicle.

"Then after that, we'll go to the Asahiyama Memorial Park," Makoto added.

"And then after that, we'll hit up the Ishiya Chocolate Factory," Nakamura continued. "And after that is the TV Tower?"

"No, the Clock Tower," Makoto politely corrected.

"That's right. The Clock Tower, *then* the TV Tower," Nakamura nodded.

"What's the Clock Tower?" Yuuki asked.

"The Clock Tower is supposed to be one of Sapporo's biggest landmarks," Kotarō explained. "It was

139

created to honor Hokkaido University."

"So what's the TV Tower?" Yuuki asked.

"It's basically Japan's version of The Eiffel Tower," Kotarō replied.

"Oh! I've heard of that one! Cool, I didn't know it was in Sapporo," Yuuki eagerly beamed.

"Wow, we've got a full day ahead of us," Daichi whispered.

"Gotta make the most of our time here," Kotarō smiled. "After all, Hokkaido was the whole point of the trip, wasn't it?"

"I guess you're right," Daichi chuckled.

The shrine was massive. If I remember right, it was the biggest of the trip. It even had a snack bar and a cafe, which, of course, we had to visit. Kotarō picked up some snacks to bring back to his family, and Oda, our resident coffee drinker, was able to get something caffeinated to drink. More power to him. If he wants to drink gross mud water, I'm not going to stop him—not that I could anymore. But even if I could have, I wouldn't have. He has already been made well aware of my disdain for the taste of coffee.

As planned, we visited the nearby zoo after the shrine. The zoo was surprisingly large and spread out. We didn't explore every single detail, as we were on a bit of a tight schedule, but we gave it the once-over, which we were all satisfied with given the summer heat. I didn't have to worry about the heat, but far be it from me to ask my living companions to suffer on my account. If I had asked, I know Daichi would have made sure we saw every little thing. But it was just nice being able to visit the zoo again after all this time.

It was about six p.m., I think, when we got to Asahiyama Park, which we forwent exploring, ha, ha, ha. We had visited so many parks at this point, I think we were all a little tired of them, but there was a spectacular view of the city from the top of it that we took some time to admire.

"I think this may be the best skyline I have ever seen," Kotarō breathed as he sat beside Daichi, and just Daichi, at one of the segmented sections of railing overlooking Asahiyama Memorial Park.

"Yeah, it really is incredible," Daichi smiled. "I think it may be the best one I've ever seen, too."

"Views like this really make you think, don't they?" Kotarō asked, his voice soft, like personified flower petals. If Minori's voice was like velvet, Kotarō's was like that of a cherry blossom petal: light, delicate, carrying an almost somber quality. It reminded Daichi, for better or worse, of the beauty of cherry blossoms.

"Yeah, I guess they do," Daichi replied. "Hey, Kotarō, since we're thinking about stuff and all, can I ask you a question?"

"Of course you can," Kotarō smiled back at the shaggy-haired boy.

"Uh, how do you know if you like someone? I asked Makoto, but if I'm being honest, I'm not sure his answer really helped," Daichi expounded.

"Huh, does this have anything to do with that love charm of yours?" Kotarō asked, making Daichi's heart quicken its pace.

"Uh, yeah, sort of, anyway," Daichi quietly confirmed. "It's just, I've never really liked anyone before."

"I see," Kotarō replied before glancing up to someone behind Daichi, but before he could get a good look at who it was, Kotarō had already shooed them off. Daichi began to make an excuse to put an end to this moment, seeing as the others must have been waiting on them, but Kotarō stopped him. "Ignore them, they're fine. We're talking. So, you want to know how you know if you like someone."

"Yeah," Daichi sheepishly admitted. He was surprised that Minori hadn't joined them but was also very grateful, as it would have definitely made the situation awkward.

"Well, let's see..." Kotarō said, looking back at the horizon. "You've never liked someone before, so let me ask, then, how does this person make you feel that's different than what others make you feel?" Kotarō smiled, returning his tender gaze to Daichi.

"Well, uh, they–they make my heart race. That's never happened before," Daichi began with a laugh. "I mean, outside when I used to get in trouble for doing something wrong as a kid."

"Okay, what else?" Kotarō warmly coaxed.

"Well, it's like...It's like I have a hard time keeping my eyes off them, you know? I had thought maybe it was just because I thought they were really cool, but...now I'm beginning to think it's just because I actually really like them, but I don't know for sure," Daichi willingly elaborated.

"Uh-huh, I see. It sounds to me like you're asking the wrong question," Kotarō replied.

"What do you mean?" Daichi quietly asked.

"Well, maybe what you should be asking yourself isn't whether you like this person but why you're questioning your feelings for this person," Kotarō elucidated. "What is it that's really keeping you from saying you like them? In my experience, when someone says 'they don't know how they feel' about someone, it's not because they really don't know how they feel. Rather, it's because something is keeping them from acknowledging their feelings."

"What's keeping me from accepting my feelings, huh?" Daichi thought out loud as he studied the skyline.

"Just a thought," Kotarō smiled. "But it sounds like you already know the answer to me."

Daichi sighed, ruffling the back of his hair. He glanced towards Minori, who was enjoying the company of his friends. *Why can't I admit my feelings?* he silently asked himself.

"Should we get going?" Kotarō asked, standing up from his place against the railing.

"Sure," Daichi chimed, removing himself from his position on the metal bars that acted as a seat.

Stop number four of our adventure in Hokkaido, Ishiya Chocolate Factory, did not disappoint. It wasn't at all what we had imagined. Certainly, parts of it were what you'd expect to see when touring a chocolate factory, but it was so much more as well. It was like someone built a confectionary and a museum inside a mansion.

There was a painted vaulted ceiling under a stone water fountain, cakes on display in glass, a grand piano! There was a foyer with a giant red carpeted staircase that parted at the top like out of a fantastical castle or something! There were model toys like planes and boats on display. They even had a metal sculpture of a skeleton on a motorcycle! The walls had crown molding, and there were stained-glass windows, ornate vintage chandeliers, glass cabinet displays of beautiful teacups. There were giant displays of how chocolate used to be made. The list just goes on and on.

It was like a visual overload. There was so much to see. It was absolutely astounding, and so much of it was unrelated to chocolate. There was even a little display for Sentai, which both Daichi and I geeked out a little over—our secret love nobody would ever know.

The "factory" was separated into five sections. There was the museum, which you might have guessed isn't a museum for just chocolate but everything and

143

anything—with no particular rhyme or reason, from what I could tell. Then there's the proper factory area, which is what one might imagine. You also have the "Chocolate Lounge," plus the store and "Candy Labo," and lastly, you have the exterior park outside, which we didn't explore. After the fever dream that is the inside of the factory, I think we were all frankly exhausted. Not only are there these five sections; each of these sections can then be broken down even further. It makes my head spin just trying to recall it all.

As I said, we didn't explore the exterior, making our last stop inside the factory the same as many people's last stop, I'd imagine: the shop…

"This place is crazy, huh?" Yuuki commented as everyone explored the candy shop, their reward after having spent what felt like an eternity seeing all the factory had to offer, from the Aurora Fountain to the Stained-Glass Room, to the Chocolate Time Tunnel and everything in between and after.

"Yeah, when I imagined this place, I definitely didn't think it'd be anything like this," Daichi smiled.

"It's almost like an antique shop." Minori replied as he floated nearby.

"I'd say it's almost a miracle we made it through everything with any time to spare," Daichi noted, glancing around the room. They had spent two hours in the factory, giving them just about an hour before closing.

"Yeah, good thing it's Oda and Makoto in charge of the planning, or it probably wouldn't have worked out that way," Yuuki laughed. "Oda is good at timing things out to a T."

"Yeah, I've started to get that impression," Daichi replied. Thinking it over, he had been the one keeping everyone on track this whole trip, making sure they got up early enough, scheduling bathroom breaks. Sure, Makoto had been the one finding things for them to do for the most part, but it was Nakamura making sure it all got done. "Is there a particular reason Nakamura is like that?"

"Oh, yeah, I guess you don't know," Yuuki replied.

"Know what?" Daichi asked.

"Oda's step-mom was in the U.S. Army," Yuuki explained, "so he and Rory are really good with time management."

"Oh, wow, I never would have guessed," Daichi replied.

"I don't think anyone would," Yuuki chuckled. "Oh, hey, here, Daichi," he chimed, handing Daichi a blue box of, presumably, chocolate.

"What's this?" Daichi asked as he took the box from the small teen. "It's that White Lovers Chocolate," Yuuki replied. "You need some, right?"

"Why would you say that?" Daichi asked, looking up from the candy in his hand. *Kotarō is the one who mentioned them, not me. Why would I need them?* he wondered as he looked at Yuuki opposite him.

"You want to confess to someone, don't you?" Yuuki asked.

"W-What? Why would you say that?" Daichi stammered, feeling his face flush.

"Makoto had asked me something about you asking me if I had ever liked someone before," Yuuki explained. "And you have that love charm. You also were talking alone with Kotarō earlier, so I just assumed you were thinking about confessing to someone."

"W-Well, that—I mean, that's not really—That's not exactly what's going on," Daichi stammered, tripping over his words.

"Oh, well, what is it, then?" Yuuki quietly asked.

145

Daichi glanced around the room, trying to locate Minori. Thankfully, he was off exploring elsewhere. It was a relief as Daichi had thought he was still nearby.

"The truth is, I'm not really sure–No, that's not it, I guess...I do like someone. It's hard for me to admit it, but after talking with Makoto and Kotarō, I don't think I can really deny it anymore," Daichi quietly clarified. His heart started to feel like it was going to burst out of his chest. But it felt like such a weight off his shoulders to acknowledge how he felt about Minori finally, even if it was scary and maybe even felt a little wrong.

But he couldn't look at it that way. If he thought of himself being gay as wrong, then he would have to admit the same thing about Minori, which he refused to believe. There was nothing wrong with Minori. Whether he was straight or gay didn't change anything about who he was. Well, aside from the obvious, like whether he would actually have a chance with him.

Not that it mattered.

It wouldn't be much longer before they had to part ways.

"You okay?" Yuuki tenderly inquired, breaking Daichi's train of thought and reminding him of the present conversation.

"Yeah, sorry," Daichi quietly replied. "Hey, Yuuki, have you ever confessed to someone?"

"Oh, yeah, all the time," Yuuki sheepishly replied.

"Really?" Daichi asked, taken aback; he didn't seem at all the type to be so forward. "Isn't it scary?"

"Well, sure," Yuuki replied. "But I guess I'm just someone who wears their heart on their sleeve. I don't like hiding how I feel from people; it's stressful. Honestly, I think it's more work than it's worth. I'd rather just have my feelings be known, and you know, whatever happens, happens."

"Thing is…I don't know that even if I confessed how I felt, it would change anything," Daichi lamented thoughtfully, looking at the square-shaped box wrapped in blue in his hand.

"You know who you really should ask?" Yuuki rhetorically solicited. "Oda."

"Nakamura?" Daichi's head snapped up. "Why do you say that?"

"Oda's the only one of us that's actually had a long-term girlfriend," Yuuki explained.

"He has?" Daichi asked, surprised that was the case. He would have been the last one he suspected of such a thing.

"Yeah, he's dating a girl who lives in America, so if anyone knows anything about liking someone, it's Oda," Yuuki smiled.

"I'm not sure he'd talk to me about it," Daichi warily smiled. "I don't think he likes me all that much."

"I wouldn't say that," Yuuki replied, appearing surprised by Daichi's response.

"I think he just tolerates me because he has to," Daichi half-smiled as he scratched the back of his head.

"Naw, I think you've got the wrong impression," Yuuki objected as he fondly smiled down at the table in front of him.

"How so?" Daichi asked.

"Well, for starters, Oda agreed to go with you on this trip," Yuuki reasoned.

"Yeah, but that's just out of respect for Minori," Daichi politely argued.

"It's more than that," Yuuki interjected, picking up a White Lovers chocolate for himself. "He picked out that charm for you, didn't he?"

"Well, yeah, I guess so," Daichi slowly admitted, not really seeing Yuuki's point.

147

"Oda isn't someone who goes out of his way just for anyone. If he does something for you, it's because he cares. Sure, maybe he agreed to this trip initially because he wanted to respect our friend's final wish, but if it were just that, he wouldn't have given you that charm. Oda, he isn't like the rest of us. He shows how he feels through actions, not words. It's just who he is. He's not a wordsmith; he's a guitarist. He speaks by doing, whether it's through music or the actions he takes. I think if you were to ask him for his advice, he'd gladly give it to you," Yuuki thoughtfully expounded, a beautiful fondness in his maccha eyes.

"What's that?" Minori asked from behind Daichi, nearly giving him a heart attack.

"Are you okay?" Yuuki exclaimed, taking a step closer to Daichi.

"Yeah, sorry, just scared myself is all," Daichi breathed. "This White Lovers chocolate, it's exclusive to Hokkaido, isn't it?" he asked quickly, changing the subject as he settled himself.

"That's what Kotarō was saying," Yuuki smiled. "I guess there's quite a few snacks and foods exclusive to Hokkaido."

"I guess you better hand me another one of those chocolates, then," Daichi smiled, extending his hand.

Daichi and the others rounded up more sweets, being sure to get stuff we couldn't get back home in Saitama. There were three specific to the Ishiya Factory: Shiroi Koibito, White Lovers chocolate; Mi-fu-yu, which were a collection of these small wafer bars; and Shiroi Baum, which looked like a circular sponge cake that was missing the center. The Shiroi Baum could also be sliced into pieces, which was convenient for us, as it made sharing a lot easier.

Poor Kotarō bought so much, I almost thought he was going to go broke, ha, ha, ha, but I guess that's the cost of having siblings to buy for.

Speaking of siblings, Oda was sure to buy some candy for Rory, seeing as he had such a sweet tooth. He didn't want to return home empty-handed, especially after visiting a chocolate factory of all places.

We left the factory just a little before closing and made our way to the Clock Tower. Though it was already night, we didn't see much of a point to not go see it. Plus, by then, we figured it probably wouldn't be very crowded.

As we had hoped, the Clock Tower was sparsely populated, and though the sky was now dark, it was lit up by a beacon of light, making it easy to see. Unfortunately, the interior was closed, but the outside was still nice to look at.

It kind of looked a little out of place surrounded by these tall city buildings, especially since it looked more like a house than an actual clock tower, as its name suggested. Sure, there was a clock and a tower, but it was just a small protrusion at the top of the red shingled roof. It was pleasant enough to look at, but of all the sights we had seen up to that point, it definitely didn't rank very high on the list.

So as you can imagine, we didn't spend much time loitering around, on account of loitering being more or less illegal in Hokkaido according to Oda. We figured it'd be best if we didn't linger.

Unfortunately, the TV Tower was closed as well. We weren't able to go up to the observation deck, so we were relegated to viewing it from the outside. I don't think any of us really minded, though.

149

"Hey, so I was thinking," Nakamura said as the group stood outside Sapporo TV Tower–The other teens shifted their attention to him, waiting to hear what he had to say–"I think we should spend another day here in Hokkaido."

"Yeah, I was thinking the same thing," Makoto agreed, his hands in the pocket of his black hoodie.

"Wait, really?" Daichi exclaimed. He wasn't opposed to the idea; he was just surprised that Nakamura was the one to suggest it.

"Well, think about it, this was the whole point of the trip, right? It'd be such a waste to only spend one day here," Nakamura elaborated. "This is supposed to be in honor of Minori right? Well, the Minori I knew wouldn't want to go out on a whimper like ending a long-ass trip to Hokkaido on viewing a TV tower from the outdoors."

"He does have a point," Minori playfully admitted. "The man knows me well."

"Yeah, you're right," Daichi laughed. "He definitely wouldn't be okay with that."

"So let's stay another day. It's not like we can't afford to," Nakamura proposed.

"Sounds good to me," Kotarō agreed.

"Yeah!" Yuuki gleefully approved.

"Okay then, let's find a hotel, settle in for the night, and then let's really explore what Hokkaido has to offer tomorrow," Nakamura said.

"Awesome," Daichi chimed. *This is great! One more day with Minori, and this time, we'll really make it count.*

Another Day...

The teens awoke bright and early the next morning at the command of Nakamura, who had taken it upon himself to plan the whole day out primarily by himself the night before, only seeking out feedback when he deemed it necessary. For the most part, the day's plans were more or less an utter mystery to the rest of the group.

After an amazing breakfast, the group set out to the stunning Hokkaido University Botanical Gardens that was only seven minutes up the road from where they were staying.

"Maybe I shouldn't be, but I'm not going to lie, I'm a little surprised that Nakamura picked this place as our first stop of the day," Daichi commented as he walked beside the stunningly beautiful Minori Saito. Even in monochrome, he was gorgeous.

"He probably just wanted a little alone time," Minori chuckled.

"Not a morning person, huh?" Daichi yawned.

"No, it's not that. He just likes some alone time after he's woken up," Minori explained.

"It's already been an hour," Daichi playfully rebutted.

"Yeah, but that hour was spent with us, so he hasn't had a chance to just...be, you know?" Minori asked.

"Yeah, that's fair," Daichi conceded. "Not like I'm going to complain. Gives us more time alone."

"Oh, Mister Takahashi, what will people say?" Minori teased as he feigned embarrassment, as if a young maiden. Even though he was joking, Daichi's heart skipped a beat.

"Oh, whatever," Daichi chuckled as he rolled his eyes. "I think we'd have bigger problems than the scandal of us being alone together."

"I suppose you're right," Minori agreed with a warm smile.

153

"I didn't expect to see so many older houses here," Daichi commented as they crossed a curved footpath boxed in by iron railings on either side.

"Yeah, me either," Minori agreed. "Pretty cool, though."

"For sure," Daichi smiled.

"You know, I've never been to a garden before," Minori sighed peacefully.

"So I'm your first, then, huh?" Daichi grinned. *Crap! Wait! That came out wrong, I didn't mean it like that!* he internally panicked.

"I suppose you are," Minori politely smiled. "I hope that's alright."

"Yeah, of course!" Daichi eagerly replied, sending his heart into a tailspin. He felt his face flush red as he gazed at the otherworldly being walking beside him.

"Good," Minori warmly replied.

"You know, *technically*, you could say your first time going to a garden was in Miyagi," Daichi posed.

"I guess, *technically*, but it wasn't *called* a garden, so I'm not sure it counts," Minori countered, thinking it over in his head.

"Fair enough," Daichi granted. "It's a win for me either way." *Shit! Was that too much? Ugh, he's going to think I'm weird!* he quickly and violently mentally chastised.

"I consider myself the lucky one," Minori casually replied.

Man, he's so cool, Daichi quietly admired as he studied the face of the boy who was paying him no mind at the moment.

"Well, look who it is!" a familiar voice chimed, stealing Daichi's gaze. He shifted his vision to see Makoto and Yuuki approaching them.

"Oh, hey, guys," Daichi politely greeted as they closed the distance between them.

"Ugh, I guess I'll have to go back to sharing you now," Minori playfully sighed, sending Daichi's heart into a stampede.

"Hey, you okay?" Yuuki asked, almost as if he could visually see Daichi's heart thumping beneath his chest. Daichi's ears felt hot; were they red? Makoto and Yuuki were going to think he was so weird!

"Sorry," Daichi sheepishly laughed. "I was thinking about something."

"Oh, was it the girl you like?" Yuuki grilled.

"Girl you like?" Minori slyly questioned, sliding his way over to where the other boys stood.

"What?" Daichi retorted. "No! No! It wasn't anything like that!" he protested, waving his hands.

"Man, your face is turning pretty red for something not involving a girl," Makoto replied with a smug smile as he shifted his weight.

"Oh, shut up!" Daichi countered.

"Anyway, we were going to start heading back to meet the others by the entrance. You want to come with us?" Yuuki asked, thankfully changing the subject.

"I'm okay; I'd like to look around some more first," Daichi politely declined.

"Alright, well, we'll see you in a little bit, then," Makoto smiled.

"Okay, I'll see you guys at the entrance," Daichi confirmed as they parted ways.

"So, tell me about this girl of yours," Minori playfully smiled as he floated beside Daichi.

"There's no girl," Daichi clarified.

"Oh? A boy, then?" Minori prodded, his voice smacking Daichi in the heart.

Oh, god, he's onto me. Wait, is he? What if he likes me and he's trying to see if I like him? Do people do that? Oh, man, what do I say? Daichi mentally consulted himself.

155

"Uh, well, to be honest, I'm not sure it really matters if there is one," Daichi explained, his eyes on the ground.

"Oh, an unrequited love, then?" Minori thoughtfully inquired.

"You could say that," Daichi half-smiled, glancing Minori's way. "Well, I won't pry, but if you ever want to talk, just know I'm here," Minori softly advised.

"Thanks, Minori," Daichi smiled.

"So, tell me, what are they like?" Minori asked.

"Stop," Daichi laughed in protest.

"Oh, come on. I promise not to be jealous," Minori teased.

"You're impossible," Daichi sighed.

The two continued to explore the gardens on their own a bit longer before returning to the entrance to meet with their friends. They were then with delay onto stop number two.

"Gojira!" Daichi eagerly exclaimed like a child as the group entered the Hokkaido Museum of Modern Art and were greeted by a very menacing, frankly evil-looking dragon-like creature.

"Oh, yeah, how 'bout that," Makoto commented, taking note of the gnarly display.

"I don't remember him looking like that," Yuuki replied, grimacing at the unsightly creature.

"Amazing," Minori breathed as he and Daichi inspected the impressively sculpted statue.

"Wow! He looks so good!" Daichi beamed.

"I can't believe he's here!" Minori exclaimed, seemingly just as excited as Daichi, which made sense as they were both Sentai and Tokusatsu fans.

Gojira was, well, "The King." At least that's what the Americans called him.

"Why does he look so weird?" Nakamura asked as he joined the two of them.

"Oh, it's because this is his most recent appearance, not counting the American film anyway," Daichi educated over his shoulder, "which I mean, why would you?"

"Daichi! There's another one!" Minori shouted pointing to the upper half of a rubber costume of the sinister-looking monster.

Daichi had been so enamored by the statue, he hadn't even noticed.

"Wow!" Daichi shouted, unable to contain his excitement. He jogged over to where Minori was floating. "Amazing! It's the suit they used in the actual movie!"

"It looks so good!" Minori squealed like a schoolgirl.

"Man, you can really tell the difference looking at them side by side. Look how much bigger his neck and head are," Daichi noted, examining the strung-up costume. "Oh, man!"

"What?" Minori asked.

"I've gotta take a picture for my dad! He'll freak!" Daichi replied quickly, taking a couple steps back and pulling out his smartphone.

"Cheese!" Minori grinned as he wrapped his arm around the neck of the costume and threw up a peace sign.

Daichi couldn't help but chuckle as he took a couple pictures, even if it was only to make Minori feel alive again. He took a quick second to send a photo to his dad, then returned his phone to his pocket.

"You want me to take a picture for you, Daichi?" Yuuki offered.

"Could you?" Daichi chimed, turning to face his friend.

"Yeah, of course!" Yuuki exclaimed. Daichi quickly

got into position with Minori. "Say cheese!" Yuuki said as he held up his phone.

"Cheese!" Daichi and Minori cheered in unison.

"Got it," Yuuki smiled. "You want to take one with the other one?" he asked, pointing back to the statue behind him with his thumb.

"Of course!" Daichi eagerly replied. Yuuki quickly took another photo of Daichi—and Minori—with the sculpted Gojira before Daichi and Minori excitedly returned to visually dissecting the costume on display.

"Man, I wish I could stay here forever," Daichi breathed as he swayed his body to see every angle of the suit from where he stood.

"Hey, we're going to go look around some more," Nakamura said from behind him.

"Oh, yeah, okay, uh," Daichi stammered as he looked back over his shoulder at the long-haired goth behind him.

"If you want to keep looking at this, it's cool. Just wanted to let you know," Nakamura casually explained.

"Uh, yeah, I think I'll stay here a bit longer," Daichi replied.

"Alright, no worries," Nakamura shrugged before walking away with the others.

"Man, you just can't beat practical effects," Daichi said as he leaned in close to the rubber costume, his arms crossed in front of his chest. "Just look at those teeth."

"Man, he's so spooky-looking," Minori said, floating around the off-putting creature.

"He's so cool-looking. I mean, my favorite design is the Heisei era, but this is really cool, too. He definitely looks scary, which is what they were going for," Daichi thoughtfully replied.

"I've always been partial to the Shōwa era myself," Minori said as he casually crossed his arms.

"The Shōwa era is great, too," Daichi chimed, motioning with a hand to Minori. "Please tell me you got to see this movie before you died."

"Of course I did," Minori chuckled. "If I hadn't, it would have been on the list."

"Fair enough," Daichi smiled. "Man, I really don't want to leave, but I suppose we should check out the rest of the museum."

"I suppose," Minori sighed.

Reluctantly, the two teens took their leave of the front lobby that housed the mighty kaiju and ventured into the rest of the museum to see what else was on display. To their surprise and excitement, it was even more Gojira—a whole exhibit, in fact—celebrating his new film.

Daichi let out an audible gasp as they entered a room dedicated to Gojira's history, where another costume stood on display. Only this time, it was the full thing from Daichi's favorite era.

"It's the Heisei-era suit!" Daichi exclaimed.

"Amazing!" Minori gleefully chimed.

"He looks incredible," Daichi breathed.

"Yeah, he does," Minori agreed as he stood atop the display, just inches from the incredible rubber costume.

"Man, I'm so jealous!" Daichi whined, watching his friend get up close and personal with the king of kaiju. He took the opportunity to take a couple photos for his dad and one selfie for himself. "This alone makes the trip worth it," Daichi noted, grinning from ear to ear.

"Easily my favorite part," Minori agreed, taking his place beside the brown-haired boy. "I don't think it's even possible to top this."

"Yeah," Daichi breathed. "I'd be hard-pressed to think of anything that could."

"And it's early, so we've had him all to ourselves," Minori smiled.

159

"I know, right?" Daichi beamed. "My dad is going to be so jealous."

"Totally," Minori laughed. "Don't be alarmed if I randomly cross over, because I think this might be the greatest day of my life."

"I wouldn't blame you," Daichi replied. "But if you're going to do that, let's wait till after we finish the exhibit."

"Deal," Minori agreed.

The two checked out the remainder of the Gojira exhibit, which admittedly wasn't much outside of some great photos and blurbs about the character throughout history. With not one but two costumes on display, though, it wasn't like anyone could expect any more; the teens were more than happy with what they had seen.

They met up with the others, and Yuuki agreed to check out the Gojira exhibit with Daichi so he could take a proper picture of him with the costume.

After they had finished seeing all the museum had to offer, they decided it was time for lunch. It was a little early in the day, but it really was as good a time as any and had been a while since they ate breakfast anyway.

Yuuki picked out a soup curry place only a few minutes away. Soup curry was a dish created in Sapporo, so it was the perfect place for them to get something to eat, and as expected, it was fantastic, really helping to hammer home the point that Hokkaido was the food capital of Japan.

Then it was back into the car for an hour drive out to the scenic town of Jōzankei, which was known for its hot springs. The teens spent the remainder of the day there exploring as much as they could, making sure to pay the Houhaikyou Dam a visit. It was then back to Sapporo for dinner, where they ate another Hokkaido special, pork-don.

"Well, what now?" Makoto posed as they exited the restaurant, they had just finished eating dinner at.

"I guess that's the end of our adventure," Kotarō smiled with a shrug of his slender shoulders.

"Not quite yet," Nakamura interjected. "There's one last place we've got to visit."

Thirty minutes away, there was a mountain—Mt. Moiwayama. That's where Nakamura led them. The last stop of the trip in Hokkaido.

Makoto drove them up the winding road of Moiwayama Kanko Expressway, where they stopped at the rope lift that a small shrine called home. They all quietly paid their respects at the wooden shrine with a seafoam-colored roof. The air hung heavy. Everyone had hardly said a word since they left the restaurant. This was it. This was the end. They had done it. They had reached Hokkaido. As that sunk in, Daichi began preparing himself for Minori's departure from this world. After this, it'd be officially over. Their last day together would meet its conclusion.

They all piled into one of the cable cars and began the last leg of their pilgrimage. It reminded Daichi of Final Fantasy X. Minori was the summoner. They were his guardians. They were there to guide him on his journey till the end of the line.

They rode in as much silence as possible, though there was an automated voice over a loudspeaker accompanied by staticky music that kept the silence from being as heavy as it was prior. Still, no one said a word.

The view from the car was spectacular as they rose higher and higher into the air, unveiling more and more of Sapporo that had been hidden by trees. It was like magic.

Upon reaching the top of the mountain, they wasted no time and b-lined it to the illuminated lookout. They lined

161

up along the dark metal railing that fenced them in, and they gazed out at a sea of gold. Sapporo looked more like the lost city of El Dorado from up here. It was golden lights for as far as the eye could see; it was the most beautiful sight Daichi had ever seen.

"We did it, Minori," Nakamura whispered, breaking the silence.

"We sure did," Kotarō choked.

"I wish you were here to see it," Yuuki frowned.

"He is," Daichi whispered, taking Yuuki's hand in his and giving it a squeeze. "I promise."

"Right," Yuuki sniffed, looking at Daichi with tearful eyes.

"Aw, dude, you're going to make me start crying," Makoto said from the other side of Daichi as he raised a finger to his eyes.

When he finished, Daichi offered him his hand. Makoto hesitated for a moment before rolling his shoulders and, with a faux cough, took Daichi's hand.

Yuuki took Kotarō's, and Kotarō took Nakamura's, and even though he could only pretend, Minori took Oda's.

They all shed some tears as quietly as possible. At least from what Daichi could hear, that's what was happening; he wasn't going to ruin their moment of mourning in solidarity to see or to even check if Minori was still with them. This was more important. He could definitely hear the heavy sniffling from Makoto and the soft whimpering of Yuuki, and he could even hear the refined tears of Kotarō, the kind of crying a mother learns to master in order to avoid worrying her children.

Daichi even felt his eyes well up a little, and when the time felt right, he slowly released the hands of his friends. Gently, the chain broke apart, allowing everyone to compose themselves.

"Let's go home," Kotarō said softly, being the first to speak.

"Okay," Yuuki quietly agreed.

"I think I'm ready for that," Makoto said, "after, you know, a night's rest."

Everyone chuckled in unison, and in the midst of the laughter, Daichi could hear Minori's voice. A wave of relief washed over him. He was still here.

"Home sounds nice," Minori said as he dreamily gazed out at the city lights, his arms resting on the railing of the lookout.

"Well," Yuuki groaned as he stretched his arms above his head. "I suppose we better get going, then."

"Yeah, it's going to be a *long* trip back home," Makoto agreed.

"They say the trip back always feels shorter," Kotarō reassuringly smiled.

"I sure hope so," Makoto laughed.

One last night together, Daichi quietly thought as he looked at the ghostly boy who paid the world around him no mind.

"Alright, let's head back," Nakamura said, his words suddenly, vividly reminding Daichi of what Yuuki had said about talking to him.

"Hey, Nakamura, can I talk to you for a second?" Daichi piped up as everyone had begun to leave. "In private?"

"Uh, sure," Nakamura acquiesced, rubbing the back of his neck. "You guys go ahead. We'll catch up."

"Alright, see you guys at the bottom," Makoto acknowledged, leading the others—including Minori, who just smiled back at Daichi, sending his heart into a flutter. This could be the last night they had together, and Daichi had to know.

"So, what's up?" Nakamura inquired as soon as the others were out of sight.

"I've been...thinking a lot lately," Daichi admitted, resting his arms on the railing beside him.

"Oh, yeah?" Nakamura asked as he joined him at his side. "What about?"

"Yuuki said you had a girlfriend," Daichi replied.

"Yeah, so what?" Nakamura sighed.

"It's just—there's this...person I really like, and I'm not exactly sure what I should do about it," Daichi explained.

"Just tell them how you feel," Nakamura answered.

"But what if there's no future with them?" Daichi quietly asked.

"What does that matter?" Nakamura coldly rebutted.

"It's just—Is there a point?" Daichi asked. "I mean, for starters, I'm not even sure they feel the same way as I do. And even if they did...we can't be together."

"I still don't see why any of that matters," Nakamura argued. "It's better to have loved and lost than to have never loved at all. Minori told me that once, before I started dating my girlfriend. Like you, I hadn't seen a point, but when he told me that...it was like all the things that had kept me from telling her how I felt—from taking a leap of faith—vanished. And all I wanted to do was try because if I didn't, then I would have spent the rest of my life wondering, 'What if…?' I don't know if we're going to last. All I know is I like her. Hell, I might even love her.

"If you feel something for this person, you should tell them, period. If you don't, you'll never know what could have been, even if there's no possible future for the two of you. I think that would make it even more important for you to tell them how you feel, because maybe they feel the same way. At the very least, then you might have the peace of mind knowing it wasn't one-sided. There's no future with them, right? So what does it matter if it turns out it was one-sided? At least you'll know and be able to move on. Takahashi, you only lose if you do nothing."

"Thanks, Nakamura," Daichi quietly replied. His words really resonated with him, but he wasn't sure he was ready to tell Minori how he felt. *I just need one more day,* he thought to himself, gazing down at the rail in front of him.

"And Takashi," Nakamura said as the wind blew through him, ruffling his hair, "just call me Oda from now on yeah?"

And with that, the journey to honor Minori's memory had come to an end.

And when we made it back from our trip to Hokkaido….

Nothing…

I think we had both assumed that once we had gotten back, I would have just magically passed on, but I didn't…I kept thinking that after I fell asleep, I would just–poof–cease to be, or at the very least wake up somewhere else. But I didn't. Days became weeks, and weeks turned to months. Summer vacation ended, and Daichi began going back to school, where I would accompany him. If I'm being honest, it was kind of nice....

I couldn't think up any more things to do, so we spent whatever free time we had just doing as couples do. We'd watch movies, go to the arcade, he even got me to sing for him, ha, ha, ha. We hung out more with the guys and his friends. We explored more than ever. We even went to this insane robot-kabuki theater thing.

Before we knew it, December had come around....

And this time, it wasn't Daichi that did the unthinkable....

It was Rory...He somehow brought everyone I cared about together–everyone. I don't know how he did it, but he managed to not only get my band to spend Christmas together but my parents as well.

Honestly, I don't know who I was more surprised by that night: my band for actually agreeing to it; my family for allowing my friends into their home to celebrate an American holiday with them; or Rory, of all people, for being the one to make it happen.

But it made me really happy. It was the happiest I had been since I died, and there in my old bedroom, looking just how I had left it all those months ago,

I finally understood...

"Daichi," Minori whispered as he looked at what was previously the entrance to his bedroom, a now glowing doorway of light, "I understand now why I haven't been able to move on."

"Why?" Daichi asked, his heart beating out of his chest.

It was the end of his time with Minori.

And now that the time had finally come, he didn't want it to end. His heart couldn't bear the thought of being apart from Minori. He had fallen utterly and hopelessly in love with him. He knew it was selfish, but he wanted Minori to stay with him even if it were just for another day longer. One more. Just one more. He began to feel sick to his stomach. This was all too much.

It's now or never.

"I love you," Minori smiled as he looked over his shoulder at Daichi behind him.

He felt a wave of relief wash over him, much like when he had come out to the boy he had irreparably fallen head over heels in love with.

Daichi's heart sank. Minori loved him? How? Why? He was completely dumbfounded. Arguably the most popular guy in his school felt the same way as he did?

"I realize now, my biggest regret in life was that I had never gotten the chance to be absolutely in love with someone," Minori illuminated, his voice like a soft caress.

"I love you, too!" Daichi blurted out, his voice trembling with each word.

"Daichi," Minori fondly replied, closing the small gap between them. The immeasurable joy he felt at those words despite their delivery was beyond description. *So this is how it feels to have one's feelings reciprocated,* Minori silently mused.

"I-I don't want you to go!" Daichi stammered, forcing the words from his mouth.

169

"I know," Minori replied softly.

Daichi's eyes remained fixed on the wooden floor beneath him. He couldn't stand to look at the heavenly figure before him. The gods had literally sent him an angel and taken him away in the same breath.

"I don't want to go either," Minori whispered as he did his best to keep smiling, his metaphorical heart bleeding with each prolonged second. *And this is the fabled heartbreak. The love songs were right after all,* Minori acknowledged.

"It hurts," Daichi whimpered, holding his chest.

"I wish I could take away your pain. I so desperately wish I could, but I can't. I can't do anything. All I can do is say 'I love you' a million times if necessary and hope that one of the times I say it will take away the pain. I'm sorry, Daichi," Minori replied as his smile faded away.

There was nothing he could do but watch the literal love of his life bear the burden of his departure. It was his funeral all over again, but this was worse. So much worse. The grieving wasn't one-sided this time. *Once again, I am an audience member at my own play,* Minori silently hissed as he gritted his teeth.

"Don't be sorry. It's not your fault," Daichi cried, trying to compose himself. *God, I bet I look like such an idiot! But I can't keep myself from crying!* Daichi internally screamed.

"Still…I wish I could do something," Minori whispered, his face taking on the look of pain, unable to reinstate his facade of optimism.

"Just give me a moment, please?" Daichi cried. *Say something. Anything. Do something! This is your doing! Fix it! Something! Daichi is in pain! Don't just stand like an idiot. He needs you to do something!* Minori screamed at himself. He wanted this misery so desperately to end, but he knew what that meant, and that alternative was just as horrible.

"Just try controlling your breathing," Minori replied, frustrated with his inability to provide a solution to the pain that plagued the both of them.

I knew this was going to be hard...but I never imagined it would be this painful, Minori quietly lamented as he watched the boy in front of him attempt to regain his composure.

Daichi nodded, tightly clenching his eyes shut as he tried to focus on his breathing and to forget about the current situation that turned him into this blubbering mess of a human being. *Come on, man, get it together. You're looking like a mess in front of Minori. Is this really how we want him to remember us? Man up!* Daichi quietly told himself in an attempt to get his emotions under control.

Minori understood now why his father had always told him to never make his mother cry. It wasn't just because it was a mean thing to do but because this was the pain he felt every time it happened. He helplessly watched Daichi cry in front of him, his face hidden from view, which admittedly did make this easier, even if only a little.

There was a long silence as the living boy tried to compose himself so he could at least look at Minori. He wiped the rivers of tears from his face and looked up at the beautiful creature in front of him. Minori looked at him with eyes of pain and a face stained with anguish.

"Okay...Okay." Daichi heaved, trying to keep it together, gritting his teeth for good measure.

"We both know I can't stay," Minori frowned, his heart aching in anticipation of the pain his words would inflict.

Daichi violently nodded, clenching his teeth harder as he tried to hold back his tears. Sensing it wouldn't be enough, he closed his eyes, his brows tightly pulling

171

together.

Daichi took several deep breaths before speaking. "I know, I know," he exhaled.

"I wish I could stay," Minori confessed again, glancing back at the doorway of the bedroom. It made him anxious.

"I know," Daichi nodded slowly, opening his eyes. He continued to avoid looking at Minori. "I just—I just wish things were different," he whined.

"Me too," Minori agreed. "I'm sorry."

"Stop saying that, please," Daichi mumbled. His words unintentionally stung Minori's heart. "You didn't do anything wrong," Daichi elaborated. "You can't help who you fall in love with; it's just not that simple, you know?"

I can't stand this! Just this once, let me do something! I don't want to leave this world as an observer! Please, just this once! the specter pleaded to whoever was listening.

"Daichi," Minori whispered, seizing his moment.

Ghost or not, he would get what he desired. He gently placed his hands on the sides of the mousy-haired boy's face. Daichi's head quickly snapped up to look at Minori, and just for a moment, he swore he could actually feel the ethereal being's hands. He was in such a daze that before he knew it, Minori was pressing his lips against his.

Though it might have just been the rampant grief wracking Daichi's soul, he could swear he felt it! In the moment, Daichi and Minori allowed themselves to give into the madness of the situation. They did not question whether or not this was real. If the passionate kisses they were sharing were nothing but figments of their imaginations, then they wanted nothing to do with reality.

No more thoughts.

Only actions.

The actions of two souls foolishly in love despite

the circumstance, in defiance of the world and laws of nature.

They would have their moment. Even if they had to force all of existence to accept it, they would have it. Alas, they couldn't escape reality long, and the impossible feeling faded just as quickly as it had appeared.

"I love you so much," Daichi whispered, his heart racing no longer from pain but excitement.

Despite their connection having been severed, Minori kept his hands where they were, his eyes transfixed on the face of his love, desperately attempting to memorize every detail.

"Daichi, you will always be my beautiful emerald jewel," Minori warmly smiled. "And I will love you for all eternity." It could have been the lingering effects of their kiss, but he swore he could feel the faint palpitations of his nonexistent heart beating.

"Promise?" Daichi asked, tears beginning to well up in his eyes again.

"I swear it on everything I know to be true," Minori passionately replied, his voice—normally like velvet—taking on a rougher quality, as though the material had been slightly worn. "I'll wait for you on the other side."

"Okay," Daichi breathed, trying his best to remain as composed as possible.

"We'll be together again one day," Minori assured.

Daichi violently nodded as tears streamed down his cheeks. *Dammit, here I go again,* he mentally noted.

"Just promise me one thing," Minori whispered as he gently placed his forehead to Daichi's.

"What?" Daichi asked, his eyes tightly slamming shut.

"Live," Minori softly replied. "Live as much as you can. For the both of us, okay?"

"Okay," Daichi whined.

173

"I won't be going anywhere. There's no rush to come back to me, so I just want you to live. Experience everything the world has to offer," Minori requested. "I want you to come back to me with more stories to tell me than I could have ever imagined."

"I will," Daichi blubbered. "I'll make you proud."

"Silly boy," Minori smiled. "I already am. Just keep doing what you've been doing."

"Okay." Daichi sniffled.

"I'm going to go now, okay?" Minori asked.

"Okay," Daichi breathed.

"Don't forget," Minori playfully reminded him.

"I won't," Daichi smiled. "Don't you forget either, okay?"

"Never," Minori swore as he pulled away. Daichi looked up from the floor to watch the lovely ghost float away.

Minori couldn't determine why, but in this brief moment, he felt okay. He was at peace. Capitalizing on this feeling, he quickly backed up to the doorway, just stopping at the edge.

One last time, he promised himself. "I love you, Takahashi Daichi," he declared as he stood at the edge of presumed oblivion.

"I love you, too, Saito Minori, now and forever," Daichi confessed, trying to keep his voice as strong and steady as possible.

With a final warm smile, Minori backed into the doorway and vanished with the light, issuing a quiet, "Goodbye, my love..."

And that's the story of how I, Saito Minori, fell in love.

AFTERWORD

I find these sections of the book the hardest to write–harder than the actual stories themselves. This one, I find particularly difficult because what you are holding right now in your hand is the second edition, a two-year journey fulfilled, a journey I had very little hand in. I originally released this book on April 4, 2021, and back then, I really didn't promote it much, or maybe I did and it just frankly didn't get very far.

I had always planned on this second edition–a version with art for every chapter, a version where someone properly went through and edited it–but I had never planned for it to take two years to do. To be honest, I just got busy with life and another project called *Pleasant Sparkle Academy: The Visual Novel.*

So I haven't really thought about *Lovely Ghost* in all that time. I'd get the artwork back and approve it or whatever, then store it away and forget about it. I wasn't really in a spot to push a new edition of the book.

And now I am, and it's a very weird headspace to be in because I feel so far removed from it. Part of me thought I could go through and tweak it up a bit, but the more I thought about it the more inauthentic it felt. I objectively *could* make it better.

When I originally wrote it, I was admittedly a little pressed for time, I suppose. I think I wrote it in four months. But for me, it's the time constraint that even allowed it to exist in the first place. Had I not given myself one and told myself to just start releasing what I had written over the years, this book would still be an ongoing project, I'm sure. Sometimes art is what it is, for better or for worse. And I think for me in this situation, it's…daunting because it's been so long and now I'm doing a proper release.

I'm scared.

Scared people will say I'm not actually good at this.

Then the one thing I've desperately clung to all these years will be taken away from me.

My worries will be confirmed: I'm not actually a good writer.

Everyone in my life has lied to me.

And that's where the constant reworking—editing over and over again—starts and then never stops. So, for better or worse, this is it. This is the book.

I'm proud of what I was able to accomplish in the time I had. I'm happy that some of the ideas I sat on for years as I tried to figure out how to tell this story finally came to fruition. I'm proud I put in the effort I did with getting my own ISBN and proud of myself for sitting down and properly designing the cover on my own instead of in some website editor.

I don't write for others. I've only ever written for myself, never caring whether someone reads what I put out. That's genuinely true. But this one, this is the first one where I've really hoped people would give it a read, even if they hated it. Even if *you* hated it, I'm thankful you gave it a chance, and I'm sorry it wasted your time, then. And to those who loved it, I hope you continue to enjoy my work for years to come, and I hope you'll take another leap of faith with the other stories I offer you.

179

Acknowledgements

I know typically you don't do both an *acknowledgements* section **and** an *Afterword* section in one book, but I just felt really compelled to. So, if you'd bear with me I'd like to acknowledge some people first I need to thank Michael Blundell for editing this book despite me taking forever to pay him for his work (much to my shame) this book would have taken even longer to happen if not for him. Next, I do need to thank my partner Alys, not necessarily for cheering me on, but pushing me to strive for more; and inspiring me by her constant pursuit of her own artistic ambitions. Without her this story I don't think would have ever been written. Next, I gotta thank Lauren Terell for being such a champion of the arts and being the first person to really want to help me get my work out there. Her enthusiasm for my work and just art in general really helped to get this thing across the finish line. And thanks to Renni Yu for doing some incredible artwork that allowed for this book to be what I had imagined in my head.